impotel..

impotent

matthew roberson

TUSCALOOSA

The University of Alabama Press
Tuscaloosa, Alabama 35487-0380

Published by FC2, an imprint of the University of Alabama Press, with support provided by Florida State University, the Publications Unit of the Department of English at Illinois State University, and the School of Arts and Sciences, University of Houston–Victoria

Address all editorial inquiries to: Fiction Collective Two, University of Houston–Victoria, School of Arts and Sciences, Victoria, TX 77901-5731

⊗

The paper on which this book is printed meets the minimum requirements of American National Standard for Information Sciences—Permanence of Paper for Printed Library Materials, ANSI Z39.48–1984

Library of Congress Cataloging-in-Publication Data
Roberson, Matthew.
Impotent : a novel / by Matthew Roberson. — 1st ed.
    p. cm.
ISBN-13: 978-1-57366-148-5 (pbk. : alk. paper)
ISBN-10: 1-57366-148-1 (pbk. : alk. paper)
1. Drug utilization—Fiction. I. Title.
PS3618.O3167I57 2009
813'.6—dc22

                    2008046372

Book Design: Theresa A. O'Donnell, Sarah Haberstich, Tara Reeser
Cover Design: Lou Robinson
Typeface: Garamond
Produced and printed in the United States of America

impotent

a novel

For Gretchen, Nicholas, and Alice

L.[1] & I.[2]

Ambien® He knew he should quit smoking.

But everyone lit up while they framed or roofed, and on breaks, and why not? The days were hot or cold, or muggy, or wet, and they struggled, morning to night, Monday to Friday, seven to seven. Not an hour passed without a cut or bruise to their hands and legs. They worked on their knees in tight spaces, drilling and nailing, and stretched to reach beams or lift lumber above their heads. They carried eighty-pound bags of shingles up extension ladders.

Why not take the simple pleasure of a smoke.

Other pleasures were gone. L. limped home nights too tired to cook a real meal, and I. didn't make dinner anymore, either, so they took out, or ordered in, or ate from the kitchen shelves—a can of olives. Six bananas. Canned chili, cold. Hot dog buns. Sex was out, except on weekends, and even then L. found he couldn't be roused. Better to watch cable. Football. Or *Die Hard*, again. He wouldn't follow tennis or soccer or any sport that looked tiring. Who needed it? He turned on baseball, in season, or listened to it on the radio, flat on his back on the living room rug.

But the cigarettes gave him a wet, morning cough, and raw, burned sinuses, and got him up from bed all night, agitated,

---

[1] Last Name, First Name, Middle Initial

[2] Insured

having to pee, and it was the nicotine—or its absence—that made him antsy. And he couldn't shit before work without coffee and a smoke, so he took them in the toilet, with the paper, and turned on the fan and drank and smoked and waited and grew hemorrhoids. I. yelled about smoking in the house but never rose early enough to stop him.

L. played lacrosse in high school. He knew what it was to be fit.

L. was not fit. He felt weathered and stiff.

He asked Dr. U_____ for something for nights, to help with sleep, but Dr. U_____ wouldn't bite. Anything he could give had risks, so he said No, quit smoking if you need to sleep, though nicely, knowing L. would take offense.

As if it's easy to quit, L. said.

He got I. to ask her doctor for a script, which she did, so they had a month's supply of Ambien, which sat on I.'s dresser. The cat knocked it off, jumping past.

The pills were white, with AMB 10 punched in their sides.

I. said this was it. She wasn't asking the doctor for more.

And Do Not Take With Alcohol, she said, because the doctor told her that was out. Contraindicated. And only one a night, I. said. There's Risk of Coma. Risk. Of. Coma. Don't be stupid.

Right, L. said.

Benadryl® Before he got the Ambien, L. tried taking Benadryl, popping back two before bed, but they wore off at three, maybe four a.m., and he would wake sweating and confused, thirsty, and mix a jug of orange juice and lie restless on the sofa.

Caffeine Mornings he knocked his way to the kitchen, where the coffeemaker sat in clutter, to brew a pot of dark blend before heading to the can (see **Ambien**).

Midmornings, he got a large coffee from McDonald's® or 7-Eleven® and stirred in sweetened creamers, if he could. Irish Crème, Hazelnut. Ditto, afternoons.

His legs shook on ladders, and a thick munge of brown coated his tongue. He had acid reflux.

Darvocet® You gotta clear the decks for eight solids, L. told Tim, about Ambien. That shit puts out the lights, he said, and even after a ten to six stretch he still floated through the a.m., his brain too slow for power tools, and his fingers coming off in the circular saw hurt like a pinch and then a tug, and then just hurt. Only two, but still. He wrapped his hand and asked Tim for his soda—the cup and the ice—and gathered his fingers and got Edward to drive him to Baptist Memorial, where they sewed him up, splinted his hand past the wrist, and made free with Darvocet. He paid the fifty-dollar fee. He went home for the afternoon.

For a while, he laid off Ambien. He had Darvocet for nights.

ex-lax® For lunch, the crew got McDonald's/Burger King®/
Wendy's®/Subway®/Popeyes®/Jersey Mike's®/Taco Bell®/
Jack in the Box®. Later, if L. and I. bought dinner, they got
pizza or fried chicken. Sometimes a salad side, with blue cheese
dressing.

L. burned it off, and I. gained weight, and got mad, and
smashed a dinner plate, and cried, because she was supposed
to sit all day and then eat like a construction worker and not
be as fat as a house? She needed L. to help. If they were going to get takeout, she said, it should be from the Kroger deli.
Roasted chicken, no skin. Or fish. Rice, and vegetables.

You don't like fish, L. said, and I. gained more weight, and L.'s
guts clogged (see **Ambien** and **Caffeine**). On the worst days,
he took laxatives and hunched through breaks in a porta-potty,
if their site had one, or on a crapper in the nearest store. At a
bodega on Fourth, L. took too long, and the owner entered, his
shoes showing through a break under the stall door. He stood
for a minute before he spoke. You all right?

Fluoride To clear the munge from his mouth and tongue (see
Caffeine), L. scrubbed with Mentadent®. Twice through his
molars and onto the front teeth and across his taste buds until
they burned.

Gaviscon® He didn't like how it foamed in his mouth, but it
helped after lunch, when burgers lodged in his windpipe and
he burped onions.

Head & Shoulders® Probably he should have used a gentler shampoo. His hair was thinning, and two shiny patches of scalp grew backward on the sides of his forehead. But he hated dandruff. He found it embarrassing.

Ibuprofen Two 500 mg capsules didn't cut the pain like Darvocet, which was long gone, ditto the Tylenol® with Codeine, and the Percocet®. It didn't help that he worked his hand all day, managing whatever didn't need fine motor skills. He lifted, hauled. He held beams while they were nailed in place. He learned to handle the nail gun with his left hand, and I. had no sympathy about the pain, because, one, he wasn't supposed to use his hand for six weeks, and, two, if he used it it wasn't going to heal right, meaning, three, he'd have more problems down the road, and, four, if he could frickin haul lumber he could get his own drink from the fridge. Put down the bag of chips or make two trips. She had enough work without having to wipe his butt, and she wasn't getting up at six anymore to help with his mornings. Maybe if he made more money, she could cut back to part-time, and she could help around the house, and they could have time for other stuff, too.

Just Tears® He gave contacts a try, because I. said to, meaning, L. knew, if she caught him popping the stems of his glasses in his mouth again, to suck off the sweat, she'd scream, but he forgot to take the lenses out at nights, and he got a corneal scratch, and glasses worked better at stopping wood chips and dust. So back to the horn-rims with a Croakies® strap.

Kaopectate® What Scott said, when he saw L. pull out a bottle, was the main ingredient was dirt or some such shit. Kao-Pectate, he said. Kao, he said. Kao-lan or lin or lon, he said. Look at the ingredients. It's clay. Bismuth subsalicylate 525 mg, L. said. Caramel, carmethylcellulose sodium, flavor, microcrystalline cellulose, purified water, sodium salicylate, sorbic acid, sucrose, titanium dioxide, and xanthan gum. Lemme see, Scott said, and L. started buying Imodium®, which came in tablets and worked better at stopping what ex-lax started.

Lamisil® The stink that came from L.'s feet when he peeled off his socks—cat piss. It was fungus and sweat. I. wouldn't let L.'s boots inside, and, when they smelled up the porch, she threw them out.

L. didn't always wear clean socks because he didn't like washing the pile of clothes blocking his closet, because that meant a trip to the basement at night or on weekends, so he ignored the mess until I. washed five or six loads and dumped clean stuff on the bed. If he wanted to sleep, he folded.

Lamisil cream would have killed the fungus, but he didn't use it regularly, most times, and when he did, he forgot to pour bleach on the shower floor, which only got clean when I. caught athlete's foot and yelled at him and scrubbed for an hour. She threatened to spend their money on a cleaning lady.

Maalox® At least it acted fast. Didn't help for long enough. Dense, like a milkshake. Chalky. (See **Gaviscon**).

Nicotine In college, when L. and I. both smoked, they could cloud a room in minutes. In L.'s apartment. Not I.'s. She didn't like how the smoke lingered in her towels and drapes.

L. bought packs of Camel Lights® for I. and left them in her coat, for her to find when he wasn't around. Matches he left, too, or a lighter, and I. always meant to do the same for L., but, absent-minded, forgot. That was okay.

When L. quit school and moved into I.'s place, they took to stepping out back, onto the balcony.

After I. graduated, she quit. She didn't want to become a pariah at work, huddling outside around sand-filled ashcans. And she needed to be healthy to have babies someday. So.

L. kept smoking with the guys at the job (see **Ambien**), and it cost more than he and I. could afford, almost thirty bucks a carton.

If L. couldn't find an ashtray or didn't want to ash in the grass, he rolled his pants and flicked into the cuffs. If there was no place to put his butts, he pinched off the red ends and pocketed the filters. Come laundry time, he and I. fought over the mess.

Oxycodone with APAP By law, he could have five days of Darvocet. After that, the doctor wrote him a script for the same thing, different name: Tylenol with Codeine. After that, a heavy dose of Ibuprofen (see **Ibuprofen**).

L. decided that for re-attached fingers, Ibuprofen didn't cut it. The guys at work agreed, and Tim scored him two dozen Percocets in original wrappers.

L. hated the stitches sitting below his knuckles. They looked like wiry eyelashes. Spider's legs. At night, before he fell asleep, he could feel his fingerbones rejoining.

Pseudoephedrine Until he dropped out of college, L. took Wal-Phed® to cram for exams and stay sharp in class and just give a lift. He lost ten pounds. He felt on edge and smoked more and wanted to smash in the heads of kids wearing sweatpants to class. Smug little cunts. Baseball caps on backwards. Never worked a day in their lives, L. figured. They could use some hard knocks.

L.'s dad said to go. He said L. didn't want to spend his life working shitty jobs. It's too hard, he said. Later on, when you get older. Look at your old man, he said. Right out of high school, roofing didn't seem so bad. For a couple of years. But use that money for college, L.'s dad said, so L. did, at 23, when he was older than most seniors. His parents bought his books.

Two years later, when he quit, they promised to help again, whenever, and I. said she would too, because they were thinking about marriage. Go back when I get a job, she said, knowing he wouldn't, and it would be a problem, someday, his lack of options. But, then again, who knew, maybe he would move up, or start a business, and she didn't want his leaving college to mean his leaving her, because she was having a tough time too, she told her mom, with classes and her major and everything, though who was she to complain.

She was lonely too often.

L. kept on with his summer carpenter position and moved in with I. He took over the rent.

About college, L. said he wanted a break. It made him itch, he said.

And he was out of funds.

Quick Pep® Only once did L. mix Quick Pep and coffee. How could extra caffeine be bad, he thought, before his hands developed a slick coat of sweat, and his heart started pounding, hiccupping every few beats, and the world tilted at the damnedest angle, and he fell to his knees, head hanging down, until he could get it together. Dropped a wallboard anchor, he said to Scott. Somewhere around here, he said. Just get another, Karl said, and L. said, Okay. Yeah.

Rhinocort® Hay fever season, four snorts in the morning. It made his nose bleed, but he didn't sneeze. It would have been better if they kept the yard down, which the lease required, but come weekends L. couldn't get himself to mow, and I. was damned if she'd do it and clip the weeds and trim the bushes, so she hired the Branski kid, David, from down the street. He did a crappy job, once a month, leaving patches of weeds climbing their fence. But there you go. If L. wanted it different, he could take care of it himself.

18

Sominex® Basically Benadryl, the pharmacist told him. An antihistamine.

Fuck that, L. said later, to I. (see **Benadryl**).

Tylenol with Codeine He kept four, for the future, for who knows what.

Unisom® Basically Benadryl, the pharmacist told him. An antihistamine.

Fuck that, L. said later, to I. (see **Benadryl**).

Valium® Dr. U_____ said, It's not a good choice. If you wake at night, cut back on caffeine. If you need help to quit smoking, we could try

Wellbutrin®, which curbs your craving.

If you still can't sleep, maybe a non-benzodiazepine. Maybe.

But not Valium, which works for intense periods of anxiety, Dr. U_____ said, like

Xanax®, which is newer. They're very addictive.

Okay, L. said. Though, at night. Even in the day. Like there's something right then. You know?

What do you mean, Dr. U_____ asked.

L. said, What do you mean?

.

L. said, Intense anxiety. Yes. I have intense anxiety.

Yasmin® I.'s doctor gave her a three-month refill, for fewer copays. She kept the extra packets in their top bathroom drawer. The pills for the month went in a soft, blue case on her dresser.

.

She needed to lose fifty pounds. The extra weight put her at greater risk for heart attack and stroke. With her luck, breast cancer, too. But she didn't like diaphragms, and she didn't trust L. to use rubbers, and they didn't have enough money for kids, and she didn't think they ever would. She'd always have to work, at least. Then, daycare costs.

They couldn't even keep a goddam house clean. No kids, she said to L. Not now, she said. Maybe never, she said. Do you care?

I. had a bank account she didn't share with L. She put away a hundred dollars a month, just in case.

Zoloft® Sometimes it's part of a bigger thing, Dr. U_____ said. The sleep. Maybe we want to think about underlying problems. Maybe you need to lift your mood.

There are a lot of good meds out there, Dr. U_____ said. Serotonin builders.

.

What's that, L. said. Antidepressants?

.

You're saying I'm nuts, L. said.

.

I don't need happy pills, L. said.

Just the Xanax, L. said. Or the other one.

I'm fine, L. said. Just fine.

Ortho Tri-Cyclen® Lo

Twice a week, instead of lunch, F.[3] drove to E.'s[4] place, where they struggled against each other in bed.

F. lost weight.

She started jogging again in the morning, before the sun and heat ruined the air.

C.[5] worried. She said F. worked too hard. She said F. shouldn't push herself. She rubbed F.'s back. She said things would work out.

She asked, Is everything okay?

F. had moved them to Oakland, to be near San Francisco, where she found work in marketing.

She led focus groups of fifteen-year-olds. She asked them to consider slogans like "Living in the Loop."

She could make a difference, she told C., letting youth culture participate in its own making. You undermine exploitation from the inside, she said, and felt foolish, but thought about

---

[3] Female

[4] Emergency Contact

[5] Cohabitant

the twenty-two hundred a month they paid for their garden apartment, and all the other expenses of life.

C. took a job at a lunch counter near Market St., so she could ride in with F. and learn the city, and meet people, and start the adoption process.

Even in San Francisco, she found it would be hard, and she spent mornings and afternoons in molded plastic chairs in offices struggling to make the most of small windows. She discussed options with agency employees, who seemed to be over thirty and less than fifty, and kind, and encouraging in the hesitant way that meant she wouldn't get exactly what she wanted.

There were kids abused or neglected by their birth parents, or disabled infants the parents didn't want to keep. There were school-age kids, and kids with brothers and sisters. There were lots of older African-American kids. There were a lot of older boys.

There were babies in Romania and China and Russia, if she could pretend to be single and straight.

Or she and F. could look into in vitro again, with a fresh eye.

At sixteen, F. dated boys. She fucked Joseph in her parents' house. He started crawling in her bedroom window, late, to stay the night.

She liked leading Christopher by the dick.

Andy ate her cunt, because she asked.

In college, she dated women, starting with Kristin, from NYPIRG, who kissed her, knowing it would be okay, and it was, and then Cynthia who she met through Kristin and Angela who she met through Cynthia.

Each of them seemed uninterested in monogamy, or long-term relationships, and they understood some things about sex men would never.

And they committed themselves to issues that mattered, because if they didn't, who would.

Right, said F. and volunteered at the Birth Control Co-op, though, for her the issue was moot.

She waitressed at the vegetarian hole in the wall.

She studied feminism and literature and wrote poetry and played Ani DiFranco and Siouxsie and the Banshees on her radio show, The CU/T.

She helped edit the alternative newspaper slash literary magazine.

She wore flaming red lipstick and bustiers.

She went out three or four nights a week.

F. felt at home.

This can't last, she told Jen, who studied accounting so she could find a job in a city that tolerated gays.

Maybe not, Jen said, which F. took to heart and applied to grad school, where she met C., who introduced her around, and recommended good classes, and cooked F. meals, and suggested, after a while, they share a place. On a trial basis, C. said. I love you, C. said.

Oh, F. said.

The Pros:

- C. knew people worth knowing. They came by the apartment to sit and talk and smoke out back. They brought wine and vegetarian samosas and other people worth knowing, and they didn't take offense when F. wanted to go to her room, though she usually hung out, and they laughed at her jokes and invited C. and F. to gallery openings and drama productions and film festivals.

- C.'s friends knew how to dance.

- C. liked color and spread paintings across the apartment in fractures of orange and yellow and red. On the bedroom ceiling, she recreated Klimt's lovers as women, in a sixty-nine, in neon.

- C. liked the reassuring rhythm of cleaning, and scrubbed the kitchen and bathroom and didn't ask F. to help.

- C.'s breasts against F.'s back. The touch of her smaller hands. Her toys, which she knew how to use. That C.

liked being blindfolded and tied while F. used a vibrator to bring her off.

- That C. hated making plans, which meant F. got her way.

- Certain things could go unsaid, though they shouldn't have.

The Cons:

- Life with another person, which to F. sounded like a prison sentence, and she felt the need for change and started fucking Brent, then stopped, and then started with Dave and stopped and refused to explain to C., who didn't ask F. to move out.

C. had fucked her share of men, too, and earlier than she should have—one two three by fifteen, when she got pregnant, and had to abort, because her mom insisted, and C.'s father understood that sort of thing happens, but not to his kid.

C. fucked men because she needed to know how a cock worked, and how to cup a scrotum, and how it would feel to have someone touching her, and inside her.

Each time, though, the sex became impractical, and complicated, and even unsafe because the boys wanted more, and she had to pry herself loose, and then her mom watched her every move.

No matter.

C. didn't attach sex to men, whom she liked only for their confidence—which turned out to be unmerited, usually, and dumb, like the boys themselves, who thought a lot about music and beer and owned scratching pubescent beards and stiff, stinking bodies, and she decided to fuck her girlfriends, who couldn't conceive of it, but who kept her attention, and her company, until she found one who had her hair spiked and used no makeup and wore coveralls and said what came into her head, like, Why don't you shut the fuck up?

I, ah, said Joseph, who hated women and ruined their lit seminar by condemning immoral texts.

Uhh, the professor said, Uhhh.

I know, Beth said, pulling her books to a pile and standing. I'm sorry. That was wrong, she said to the professor. I'll go, she said, and later to C., who searched her out—What a douchebag.

C. said, You want to get lunch?

C. found that a woman could slide her legs between C.'s.

A woman could gently lift C.'s knees back against her chest.

She could brush the sides of C.'s breasts and the tips of her nipples.

She could use her fingers and tongue.

And. C. could do the same until she felt Beth's hips lift, her muscles contracting around C.'s hand, and she would have done it forever if Beth hadn't told her to get a life.

You're too needy, Beth said.

Beth said, Don't call me anymore.

What's wrong with having needs, C. said, though the line was dead, and then she cried until her arms hurt.

E. knew about C., because he asked.

This is just about sex, F. said, after their first time, after coffee, after how many years. You and me, she said.

I didn't know you'd moved out here, E. said.

Jennifer told us to look for you, F. said.

You and C., E. said.

Me and C., F. said.

F. needed her life full, because anything less felt frightening, like being lost in the middle, and no one would fill it for her, she thought, unless she made them.

F. called herself ambitious and worried she was greedy and couldn't explain the difference.

F. worried about the future. She worried about C. What C. wanted.

F. worried she was too old for a kid. Too selfish, and she didn't like noise.

What kind of animal shits itself?

But more life.

E. took his job when a friend recommended him to a friend. The firm offered dental. He took the first apartment at the right price.

E. ate sandwiches or omelettes or steaks from restaurants near where he felt the need. He bought his clothes online, from Levis.com® and The Gap®, when he couldn't write more code. He owned a rowing machine and weights for late at night or early, if he woke.

In his twenties, after the army, he planned college and a career and marriage and a family. After his divorce, he took a useless major and tried grad school, and then medical school, and then he retrained in computers. Now, he went to movies and drinks with friends, and owned a PlayStation®, and sometimes he found a fuck in a bar. Once in a while he called an escort service. He put his extra cash in mutual funds. Why not, he thought, and only felt bad when Eric, at work, complained about his kids, because Eric didn't mean it, not a word. Not about the laundry or the wasted food or getting up nights.

Eric's smile.

When F. came to hand, E. thought again about what he wanted, though he knew better. Things didn't work out for him, and F. lived with C., and she wasn't one for the long term, and she told him, month after month, it just—that it didn't mean anything. Them.

Maybe E. loved F., whatever that meant.

I don't think so, F. said, and skipped two weeks seeing E., and then came back, and found him at the apartment, waiting.

F. asked Dr. ------------- for birth control pills, but didn't take them.

I miss you, C. said. Where are you, she said.

Their first year, F. bought C. flowers. She drove C. to antique shops and rummage sales and surprised her with a trip to New York, and one to New Orleans, for Mardi Gras. She drew C. hot baths. She signed them up for ballroom dancing class. She posed nude when C. asked, sometimes for hours.

Then every year after, F. did the same, or the same sorts of things, even if sleeping somewhere else.

It's a largeness, C. said once, explaining, to Susan. She's a big person.

And that makes you what, said Susan.

I don't know, C. said. I'm me.

Still, C. felt small, and she suffered the nights F. stayed with Brent or Dave, and she left the apartment when F. returned distracted, smelling of metallic sweat and semen, her hair loose.

It's me she comes back to, C. said. She doesn't lie to me, C. said. It's never another woman. She loves me, C. said, and she did.

F. had said that when they moved across the country, to San Francisco, they should have a child. F. said it.

C. couldn't have cared for a baby at fifteen, but she would have loved it, nonetheless.

F. liked smoking in E.'s place, because he hated it. She threw her clothes across the floor.

She tore the sheets off E.'s bed when they fucked, and, later, she watched him tighten the corners and lay the pillow across the top.

She liked kissing him after sucking his dick, especially if he'd come. Sometimes she slapped him or pulled his hair. She told him she'd bring a strap-on and fuck him in the ass and slipped her finger in there when he turned her sideways and lifted her leg and pushed himself in.

If you say it's over, he said. I won't be here next time, he said, though F. knew he would.

It's over, F. said.

You're sure, E. asked.

Can we talk, C. said.

I went to the international agency today, C. said.

They seem good, C. said.

F., C. said.

.

I'm pregnant, F. said.

Oh, C. said.

Is it mine, C. asked.

What do you think, F. asked.

A.[6] & P.[7]

A. After grad school, A. temped. She learned that: 1) Business is soulless and 2) Its employees—the same.

That's what she said, anyway, and she had examples—building contractors and auto dealers. Enron and Disney.

She said business sucks, because money rules.

People say stupid things like "ramp up" and "step up to the plate" and "proactive."

She said, The women act nasty and the men want to be tall. Like high school.

And every last one knew how to put her down. About insecurities they were smart.

One boss stared at her boobs. When A. wore baggy shirts, he called her professor. He said she'd make a great teacher, which meant she'd failed as a writer slash copyeditor slash file clerk slash receptionist. Like she wanted that.

A. wanted to make an impact. A difference.

So what do I do, she said to P.

---

[6] Agent

[7] Partner

How about a nonprofit, P. said.

Yeah, A. said. Okay.

I think they say not-for-profit, A. said.

P. P. studied chemistry, and he wanted industrial work, where he wouldn't write for grants, or teach. P. liked the lab. He liked state-of-the-art. He liked the salary.

He went to work for Dow, in the middle of Michigan, in Nehrke's lab. He found his boss had a sense of humor he'd have to endure.

When P.'s first project dried up, Nehrke said the people upstairs wanted to abandon all current efforts.

But P. would always keep his job. He could be of use on many tasks.

Even on weekends, P. smelled like chemicals, even his breath. A. worried about his lungs.

P. took an interest in their new yard, planting bulbs and hedges and mulching, and he decided to build a white picket fence from scratch.

He talked to A. about getting a new car, and/or a truck, to tow a boat, which he wanted to be at least nineteen feet, so they could weekend at Higgins Lake.

He bought a weight machine for the basement and worked out for the first time since high school, when he wanted to look like Tarzan.

He signed up for a class in Shaolin Kung Fu—the northern tradition. Not the southern.

K-Y®

And A. thought about babies, which she didn't want, and did. Want.

What didn't she want.

A. didn't want diapers, or the laundry.

She didn't want the cost of clothes, or stained hand-me-downs.

Rummage sales with deals on broken toys.

She didn't want to breastfeed or fight over food.

What if the kids hated baths? What if they hated her?

P., the kids would love for sure, like everyone, and A. would play the villain, like her Mom.

Maybe she'd be out of the house, with a career. But she didn't want daycare.

She'd get fat and constipated and moody and have hemorrhoids and bladder problems. Her skin would stretch. Her vagina.

She'd get a clumsy epidural and be paralyzed.

The pain of birth.

But a warm little bug.

A. wanted.

And a family of her own, to be with her, in one way or another, for the rest of her life.

Let's get pregnant, A. said.

She didn't want the sex.[8]

---

[8] The label that one doctor and then another offered was Dyspareunia. The label didn't help, because it meant painful intercourse, and A. didn't need a label. She needed a solution, which Dr. One couldn't provide, because, he said, it wasn't a physical problem, but psychological, which led to physical discomfort. He said she needed to loosen up, which A. told P., who said, What? A. said, there's no trauma or infection, so it's me being uptight, which comes from stress, and we should practice relaxation. But he didn't say loosen up, P. said, and A. went to Dr. Two, a woman, who said:

> If your parts seem healthy and you're lubricating just fine, and your PC muscles aren't contracted and intercourse still hurts, the treatment may be slightly longer term. The pain you're feeling may be due to vulvodynia or vulvar vestibulitis syndrome, and treatment may involve: Local anesthetics

Clomid®

The problem with wanting, A. knew, is getting. For everyone, P. said, but A. didn't believe it, and she ticked off one two three four five of her friends with careers and babies and two cars under ten years old. Yeah, P. said, but who really knows, and, he said, think about •••• and ••••••• and •••. Things for them, he said, things aren't good.

They're not barren, A. said, and P. said   , because he knew A. knew she wasn't barren, whatever that meant.

He thought to say chill out. It would make A. yell, and so would P. Then A. would slam cupboards. P. would kick the wall.

or topical creams or sitz baths to help alleviate the pain or biofeedback therapy, which can teach you to enter a relaxed state in order to decrease pain sensation and/or antidepressants such as amitriptyline (Elavil®). <http://www.elavil.com/>

It's in my head, A. said.

She said to loosen up, A. said.

She said that, P. said.

She said join a support group for hysterics who've suffered sexual trauma.

What, P. said.

Or I can participate in a research study examining treatment of vulvodynia and vulvar vestibulitis with Botox®.

I'll buy some K-Y, A. said. She felt too mad to cry, though she did.

They'd make amends, roughly, in a way that wouldn't feel like the insertion of part 1 into slot 2 for production of emission 3 in hopes of baby 4.[9]

But P. leaned toward pacifism, because he liked being a thoughtful guy, and people liked him for it. So he said

and puckered his lips in compassion, and empathy, and looked at A.,

---

[9] These things, P. thought.

How thin skin feels.

His coppery sweat, and the tangy smell of A.

How she turned away from his stubble.

The press of air when he entered.

His aching elbows. A. pushed him off her breasts.

The itch in his thigh.

The routine.

Her lips.

And he shifted and with one hand cupped the flesh at the base of her spine and raised her hips and pushed in again and again and thought of turning her, of fucking her from behind. Of twisting her hair in his fist.

He didn't.

Want.

To fuck.

Did A.

A. seemed happy, waiting to see.

who suffered from a luteal phase defect, according to Doctor
Three, who assured her that it remained

> a commonly misunderstood condition that frequently affects
> fertility. If a patient can produce a luteal phase longer than 10
> days, a pregnancy can be sustained. This can be achieved
> through progesterone supplementation, Clomid, which fools
> the body into believing that the estrogen level is low.
>
> This altered feedback information causes the hypothalamus
> (an area of the brain) to make and release more gonado-
> tropin releasing hormone (GnRH) which in turn causes the
> pituitary to make and release more FSH and LH. More follicle
> stimulating hormone and more luteinizing hormone should
> result in the release of one or more mature eggs—ovulation.
> <http://infertility.about.com/cs/clomi1/a/Clomid.htm>

Whoopee, said A., who got sonogram after sonogram before
the intrauterine inspections charting her follicle production.
She got blood tests, too, from a wattled nurse who missed
veins and left bruises on the insides of A.'s elbows.

A. and P. would have a six-month treatment window, after
which other, more complicated options could be pursued, if
necessary.

Won't we have twins, P. wanted to know. Isn't that what
happens?[10]

---

[10] Twin pregnancies may occur in as many as 5% of the women who use Clomid. Triplet pregnancies are far
more rare. Other reported adverse effects include ovarian enlargement 13.6%,Vasomotor Flushes 10.4%,
abdominal or pelvic discomfort, distention or bloating 5.5%, nausea and vomiting 2.2%, breast discomfort
2.1%, visual symptoms (blurred vision, lights, floaters, waves, unspecified visual complaints, photophobia,
diplopia, scotoma, etc.) 1.5%, headache 1.3%, and abnormal uterine bleeding (intermenstrual spotting, men-
orrhagia)1.3%. Although there has been much talk about the relationship of clomiphene (and other fertility
drugs) to ovarian cancer the vast majority of the evidence now seems to point at infertility itself, rather than
the use of fertility drugs as being the primary explanation for the slightly increased incidence of reproductive
cancers in the infertility population. (See recent discussion on our boards.) <http://infertility.about.com/cs/
clomi1/a/Clomid.htm>

What happens.

Pregnancy Plus® *

Into the second trimester, A. woke P. She pressed him to the mattress. She bent forward on one arm. She put her breasts to his mouth.

P. wondered.

Sometimes he said no, to the breasts, feeling they weren't for him.

Sometimes he said no, to the sex.

But A. said, Dr. Heinle says we should enjoy all the sex we can. And she said Dr. Heinle said, Lucky P.

P. didn't think obstetricians should joke about their clients' sex lives.

The sight of pregnant women started making him hard.

A. bought books, which she left on the coffee table, or on P.'s desk. So he could study.

They were no substitute for experience, but they'd help.

P. read none, stacking them instead on a shelf. He spent his evenings watching TV, the sofa cradling his prostrate hump.

A. read her assignments in the chair next to him, her feet up past the lift of her stomach. Did she look his way?

* You Should Take Prenatal Vitamins!!
Both you and your baby need plenty of vitamins during pregnancy, and by taking special prenatal vitamins you guarantee that you are getting everything you need. Getting the proper vitamins can also help you avoid diabetes. <http://www.bygpub.com/natural/pregnancy.htm>

Dilatation and Curettage*

After the miscarriage, A. knew they'd try again, though the baby, mostly formed, had been missing a brain, had been hopeless from the start, which meant their excitement had been pointless, stupid, and A. felt sick. Embarrassed. Ashamed.

They decided to remember the baby as H., and A. started plotting her cycles.

To P., who was spooked, A. offered literature that said one fetus with a defect didn't mean a thing, and they were under forty, and, though they'd had trouble conceiving, she said, there was no problem. She was healthy, she said, and he was healthy, and if they took fertility measures, everything was normal, and they could have a baby. She wanted a baby. He did, too, she said, and she wasn't wrong.

I'm just, P. said. What if there's another problem. What if you miscarry?

What if it has a problem, he said.

He won't, A. said, who knew he wouldn't, somehow, maybe through strength of will, because she wouldn't live her life without a child, not when they had a house and money, and they could make the time.

There's adoption, P. said, and told John, later, A. wants one. We're trying again, he said, and looked along the bar.

The doctor says fine, P. said.

The doctor brought it up, P. said.

She said a situation like ours. H. It doesn't mean anything, P. said.

John said, That's great. Good, and he studied the foam in his glass.

Yeah, P. said. That's what she said, P. said, and thought about ultrasounds, which missed a whole lot, and professionals who only knew the odds, no matter what they said, and he'd always known a baby would be hard, but this was hard.

A. really wants one, P. said.

Where do they get this shit, John said, pointing at the weathered sleds and skates and skis and wagons and bikes and lanterns hanging around the restaurant. They've got the same stuff in every one.

---

* i.e., uterine scraping.

Trileptal®

Try again.

A. brought pens to her new job, and Post-Its®, and they disappeared.

It's not like I leave them out, she said to Dot. I put them in my drawer, which I close, A. said. Like this. Open, she said. Closed.

No one knows you paid for them, Dot said. She scratched her cheek. They need pens. Share and share alike, she said, though Dot kept her pens in her purse, with her notepads and her hole punch. Sometimes she had paper clips.

You shouldn't spend your money, Dot said.

And I write with what, A. said, blood?[11]

A. expected fellowship around a common cause.

---

[11] Sometimes A. saw husks of supplies on the workroom counter—an empty box of Bics or binder clips—but never their contents. Once she saw wrappers for two reams of paper and plastic cellophane that had covered what, notepads? When she saw them, she saw them at eight a.m., bright and early and still too late.

She tried asking Jenny, because it was Jenny's branch, after all, but Jenny said, Priorities, A. We do what we can, she said, and disappeared behind a door.

I just want to know who's in charge of supplies, A. said, to the air.

She got Keith, whose Cheetos® fetish left orange crud around his lips, and whose shirts all missed buttons over the gut.

Dot said, His mom works upstairs. She manages Michigan. He could not keep anything else, she whispered.

And A. got Tom, in his fifties, in cardigans, who apologized. His reports, he knew, they could be more concise, and the office, he knew, it could be more efficient, and the world, well, A. learned not to get him started. It could be a better place, he said. Well, he started, Well, or, I know. Yes, I know. Right, right, he said a lot. Or, Now. Now, he said. A. wanted to meet his wife, his kids, but she never did.

Dot said Tom wanted to manage their branch. He never got it, she told A., the job, as if A. didn't know. He takes it very well, Dot said. No kidding, A. said back.

Henry wore a flat-top from his time in the marines, in the 70s, before the end of the draft, but after new soldiers shipped to Nam. Henry said Nam like he'd been there. About Nigeria, where he'd worked later, as part of the Human Rights and Justice Group International®, he only said, They got some problems. Tough on the kids. It got him into helping youngsters, he told A. He used the word youngsters. He clocked in at eight a.m. and out at four and ate a sack lunch at his desk. In wet weather, he carried a golfing umbrella big enough to cover patio furniture.

He is a good man, Dot said, and though A. didn't know what that meant, she agreed, because she had no other response for a woman who commuted in sneakers. Who spoke without the use of contractions. Who used the word "oopsie." Who read the manuals for new office equipment. Who'd spent the last ten years pursuing a master's degree in curriculum and instruction. A. didn't know what curriculum and instruction meant, and she hadn't known an M.A. could take ten years.

Jenny told A. the office would collapse without Dot. Everyone relies on her, Jenny said, including me, she said, fresh from her program in public health.

Everyone would still rely on Dot, A. knew, after Jenny passed through to manage some larger office in a real city.

There's ambition at the top, A. said, to P.

A. provided web content. It described the mission and vision of LifeLight. It offered frequently asked questions from birth mothers and adoptive parents alike. A. culled testimonials from satisfied clients and organized them into a narrative illustrating the agency's quality and conscientiousness. She described with the right detail both their domestic and international programs. She learned to link the phrase "loving home" with the phrase "full disclosure" (because, after all, most of their kids came from China and Russia and Ukraine and Kazakhstan and Guatemala, and their clients, knowing little else, understood conditions there, for orphaned little girls, failed to reach substandard levels). She provided links and resources on adoption, and she managed the agency's online application forms. She fielded email inquiries. She took the title Webmaster, though a musty-smelling boy from the tech school handled real programming.

Jenny called her the WebMistress.

Then, like everyone else, A. took on other jobs, because they needed to be done but LifeLight couldn't hire anyone new. She handled the paperwork sent in by international adopters—the I-600A Application to Immigration (the orange form), the I-864 Affidavit of Support, and the tax returns and birth certificates and marriage certificates and divorce decrees (if applicable) and fingerprint forms required by the INS. She became a notary public.

Sometimes she answered phones.

She learned to unjam copies and the fax machine.

A. didn't handle: 1) Clients and 2) Money.

Those stayed the territory of Jenny or Dot or Henry or Tom.

Why, A. asked Keith.

I don't know, he said.

Keith knew nothing. A. thought he probably made the most, too.

A. learned that not one American child under the age of five went through the agency without something like Joubert Syndrome or microcephalia[12] or cerebral palsy. Every one had what the adoption community called developmental delays.

A. learned about incompletely closed spinal columns. She learned about seizures. She learned about G-Tubes for feeding. She learned that children can come with abnormal heart placement.

Some days, A. felt like her heart was abnormally placed, finding a home in her arm or her stomach or her throat, anyplace but where she wouldn't notice the insistent pulsing.

She told P. it had as much to do with those kids as her knowledge that she'd never, ever take on, and I quote, she said, the work of a baby needing a family strong enough to give him a normal, healthy life and be prepared for his future prognosis.

That's what I write, she said, to P. Things like that.

They would save and borrow and join numbers of efficiently-packed middle-class Americans traveling to orphanages in countries they'd never visit on vacation. If they had to, A. told P.

---

[12] microcephaly • mi cro ceph a ly or mi cro ce pha li a • noun;

Definitions: small head: the condition of having a small head or having reduced space for the brain in the skull, often associated with learning difficulties mi cro ce phal ic adj

P. said that Colm Freed, in plastics, had a little girl, Chinese.

P. said that Colm said he and his wife spent a few days with villagers before returning home.

The villagers, P. said, They couldn't understand Americans taking a Chinese baby.

It upset them, P. said. That's what Colm said.

Upset them, A. asked. Chinese families discard their little girls, A. said. In dumpsters.

A. said, They've got thousands of orphanages full of little girls that never get held.

They could give away a million babies, she said, and not shrink the population one percent.

A. asked, Did what'shisface tell them that?

I guess not, P. said.

A. said, Colm.

Yeah, P. said. C.O.L.M.

No one at LL asked A. a thing, but they all knew about her, the way people do.

They knew:

A. had never before given willingly of her time.

That A. didn't donate money, unless on the spot.

That she hated rallies or group efforts of about any kind.

Strong beliefs seemed unreasonable to her, even when they made sense.

She only gave to Goodwill for the tax break, padding the value of her junk.

That her father made six figures, and her mom stayed home, redoing some part of the house every year. That her family voted Republican and wanted success for her, though they couldn't say what kind.

They knew A. thought she deserved something, though they thought she knew better than that, too.

Tom said he felt it early. When he was a kid. A call. People need help, he said. And I knew I should, he said. Help. I liked it. Like it, he said.

I was one of ten guys in the social work program, he said. At UConn. Ten men. There were a couple hundred women, he said.

That changed, though, he said.[13] The numbers. It was the seventies.

People were committed, Tom said.

They still are, Tom said. Nobody notices, he said, but we're still out here.

Everyone I know, he said.[14]

My wife, he told A., helps people with disabilities find work.[15] My sister, Joan, and her husband, they teach in Chicago, in the city, he said. His friends from college, he told A., they work for the Peace Corps, he said, and AmeriCorps, and his friend, Roger, he's a Unitarian minister. He was a public defender first, Tom said.

There's a lot of burnout, he said.

People switch around, he said.

But I don't know anyone who's given up,[16] he said.

---

[13] He says a lot changed back then, A. said, to P.

Yeah, P. said. Like the price of gas.

[14] Everyone I know, P. said, works seventy-hour weeks and makes six figures. People in my lab drive forty-thousand dollar cars. They eat out. They take nice vacations. They invest. I'm just saying, P. said. That's the norm. Maybe things changed, P. said, but they changed back.

I'm not saying it's right, P. said. You know that.

[15] It's how you say it, A. told P. Saying disabled people puts disabled first, people second. So you say a person with disabilities. It's important, A. said.

[16] I don't think I'll ever do anything else, A. said.

You can't give it up, he said. It feels good. We do good, he said, to A.

I know, A. said.

After Christmas, Henry asked, You want to work with a mom?

She's nineteen, Henry said, and she's in her fourth month. She goes to college. She's pro-life, Henry said.

She wants to place with a heterosexual couple, he said. She wants support until the adoption. Some living expenses. She wants medical expenses, legal expenses, and travel.

She wants to choose the parents.

She wants pictures and letters. She wants the child to know her. To know of her, Henry said.

She doesn't want the baby, Henry said.

I mean I don't think she consented. You know? She didn't really say.

She's going to need someone, and the adopting parents, too. It's a commitment, Henry said. For a good half a year. They're gonna count on you.

You can use Sandy, in counseling, Henry said, and I'm here to help, and Tom and Dot, but it's yours, finally. You're the go-to girl. The coach. There are a lot of ups and downs. I get calls in the middle of the night, Henry said. Scared moms. Anxious parents. Half the time it falls through. A lot of emotion, he said. You gotta be tough.

It's more than a full-time gig, you know?

Jenny said, later, We don't even let the new counselors take a case until they've been here maybe three months.

Over lunch, Dot said she started part-time, as a secretary. Then I got involved, she said, and they saw I wanted to help. That was before Henry, even, Dot said. And I could do it, Dot said. It's not the education, she said. It's being organized. It's caring about the clients. They become family.

Tom said he felt sorry that they couldn't pay her more for the work, not at first. Maybe later, if it went well. Meantime, he said, there's other satisfactions.

This might be one of the most important things, ever, in the lives of the parents. And the mom and the baby, Jenny said.

You want it, Jenny said.

I want it, A. said.

Think it over first, Jenny said.

I'm going to have to pass, A. said.

I can't do it, she said.

I'm pregnant,[17] A. said.

Weird timing, she said.

I guess I'm giving notice, A. said. Seven months.

If it goes to term, A. said.

---

[17] again

Digitalis[18]

Dr. ~~~~~~ said the triple screen warranted another sonogram, Just, he said, to see. There's no cause for concern, he
said. Let's just check. Even then, he said. You get false results.
The only sure way, Dr. ~~~~~~ said, is an amnio, because we
missed the window for a CVS. Or we can do a PUBS, which is
more accurate. But it carries more risk.

What, A. said.

A what, P. said. What?

I've got materials you folks will want to read, Dr. ~~~~~~
said. Then you'll want to talk it through. But let's not wait too
long.

And let's not worry, Dr. ~~~~~~ said. Okay?

Oh, P. said.

It's because I'm old, A. said. Isn't it?

I don't need to read anything, A. said.[19]

---

[18] Timely surgeries for cardiac and gastrointestinal anomalies in Down Syndrome babies are necessary to prevent serious complications. Digitalis and
diuretics are usually needed for the medical management of cardiac anomalies along with prophylaxis for subacute bacterial endocarditis. <http://www.
emedicinehealth.com/down_syndrome/page5_em.htm>

[19] A. already knew about abnormal chromosomes, and operable heart defects,
and the chance for infection and for respiratory, vision and hearing problems
and thyroid conditions. She knew she and P. would spend twice their time and
money on care, and the rest of their lives.

And the baby's life. How hard would it be.

And I'm not having an amnio, A. said.

So what if we find out, A. said.

It doesn't change a thing, she said.

We're having this baby.

I don't care, A. said.

I don't care, she said, looking at P.

P. said,

....

You guys take a little time, Dr. ~~~~~~ said, and give us a call.

I'm having this baby, A. said.

I know, P. said.

Okay, he said. It's going to be okay, he said.

Come here, he said. Okay, he said. Okay.

And we don't know, P. said, for sure.

I know, A. said.

M.[20] & S.[21] & C.[22] & C.[23]

M.'s boss wore muumuus to work. She weighed two hundred pounds. She shouted a lot.

They called her Jabba. The Hutt.

Jabba wanted ◀↑⇨↖↕⇦⇦↕↔⇨△↓→↑◀, and she wanted it NOW.

M. had no clue. He felt stupid.

He gritted his teeth. His stomach hurt through to his back.

Needed: Experienced writer and editor. Must know higher education. Our company provides positioning campaigns for colleges and universities who need to represent their true selves.

M. wrote slick copy for slick brochures.

M.'s copy went in a product filled with glossy shots and taglines.

---

[20] Male

[21] Spouse

[22] Child

[23] Child

But, first, they niggled over proofs—over colors, which could be a shade darker lighter more blue red green, and the shots, which should be cropped in tight.

Or Jabba said the word "inspired" feels religious, so find another, or use it more, for the Christian schools, and don't leave widows.

They sold add-ons, like market surveys and web designs, for fifty grand more.

They worked to develop lifelong relationships, which meant more money from the following:

A: the clients and
B: the clients' cohorts.

And M. ate shit until the boss was satisfied. Her name was at stake, right?

She hated him, which M. didn't understand.[24]

Jabba was an ENFP[25] on Myers-Briggs.

---

[24] It was M.'s first real job, his first real boss.

[25] Extroverted Intuitive Feeler with Perception (as opposed to Introverted Sensing Thinker with Judgment).[1] AKA a "Big Picture Person." AKA works from the gut. AKA emotional to an extreme. AKA can sniff the wind.

[1] Designed in the 1950s, Myers-Briggs's multiple choice questions (questions designed in the 1950s that focus on one's comfort level in crowds and the neatness level of one's "workbench") determine the Jungian archetype most applicable to a given individual, i.e., they tag a test taker as having four of eight essential traits, with subordinate subtraits, i.e., they label personalities into tidy categories for use by administrators who take metaphors for essential truths, condemning the poor schmuck taking it, thought M., to life as the sum of his letters.

More like CUNT, Ron said.

M. shrugged.

M. felt hopeless.

The pay was great.

S. Here's what S. wanted:

A career	Family
Authority	The necessities
Independence	Hobbies
Money	Love
Power	Happiness

S. didn't believe in changing the world, not a corner. Nothing changes, and people behave badly, and you fight for everything.

You need to care for yourself, and earn a wage.

Take no shit, particularly from your husband, if you have one.

Don't compromise.

Don't be foolish. Don't waste your money.

Be educated.

Work hard.

But have a family: one, two, maybe three kids. Spend your days raising them well. They should be smart and kind.

Attend to their feelings.

Their father. They must have a close relationship with their father. So could you.

Do things together, at the zoo, and the park. Make time and spend it.

Knit in the evenings, when you can.

S. liked shopping. She ordered catalogs from a website called catalogs.com. She made online purchases, and, in her spare minutes, browsed eBay.

She taught full time.

She wrote articles on mothering.

She took care of the kids and the house, and it was a job and a half, and she was tired.

Her parents sent extravagant gifts and helped them buy a house and car.

M. and S. had a child.

Before they got over the shock, they had another.

S. said she wanted three, and M. said he'd leave.[26]

To start labor, doctors use needles to puncture the amniotic sack. If meconium spills out, the baby has defecated, which suggests distress.

They felt it, too. The distress.

Then the garbage bag rolled under the table to capture blood and shit and tissue.

---

[26] No more children, he said. We're too old. We can't handle two. We don't have any money. I need sleep.

Vasectomies, he discovered, can be done in an hour. He wouldn't have to tell. Then, he thought, whatever she wants. Another kid? Sure. Try all you like.

Eventually, the knife.

Episiotomy: "…is an incision into the perineum (area of skin between the vagina and the anus) to enlarge the space at the outlet."

Human Labor and Birth, Fifth Edition, Harry Oxorn.

Image: Robin Elise Weiss at <http://childbirth.org>

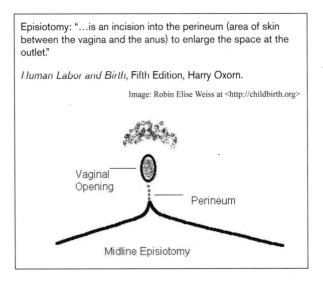

For C., a nurse climbed on the table and pushed S.'s stomach. The doctor used forceps.

S. screamed.

M. hid in a corner.

It went no better with C.

Babies.

Babies take over a house.

They won't sleep. They need bouncing, and want to be held.

They poop themselves.

M. and S. comforted and rocked and fed and changed.

M. and S. tiptoed at night, careful of creaks, next to the wall and on the tile. From bed to the bathroom.

M. oiled door hinges. Then the doors swung at a touch, only stopping when they smacked a wall.

Don't touch the doors.

M. peed sitting down, which was quieter. He didn't flush.

They moved the TV to the back room, turned off the phones, and the answering machine. The microwave they stopped, always, before the beep.

They hushed the dog, and took his collar off to stop the ringing tags.

They didn't bang the dishes, drop their shoes, laugh, or yell.

They talked in whispers, when they talked.

And the following:

They washed babies, dried babies, walked babies, hugged babies, rocked babies, cradled babies, wrapped babies, swung babies, dressed babies, shushed babies, changed babies, lifted babies, fed babies, rolled babies, hugged babies, tipped babies, wiped babies, bobbed babies, checked babies, cooled babies, burped babies, warmed babies, patted babies, hugged babies.

They applied ointment to rectums and rashy skin. They bathed through crying, and smoothed on lotion, and brushed hair. They cleaned the gunk from under C.'s foreskin. They trimmed fingernails, toenails, and syringed snot from noses. They wiped off curdled-milk vomit, and staunched drool. They cut hair. They applied eyedrops. They forced down the pink medicine. They did things that made the babies cry. You have to do the tough stuff, M. thought. Someday the kids would know that.

They went for walks.

Sunday mornings, the park, with its wide, paved paths. C. in a stroller. C. in a sling. The dog.

They draped blankets to keep the sun off the stroller and lifted it over curbs and bumps.

- Always bring toys.

- Don't go too far, because, when something goes wrong,[27] you have a long walk back.

---

[27] No diapers, of course.

And colds. Ear infections, and fevers, and C. cried, miserable, hot and snotty. His eyes caked over. He smelled of metal. They took him to the doctor, in the day, and to the emergency room at night, when his temperature grew.

You can't fuck with fevers, M. said, as if he knew, and lifted C. from the crib and into his car seat. M. tucked a blanket around the edges.

S. watched, their dinner on the table. You eat, M. said.

M. left the car to block an ambulance lane. He jumped line at admissions.

So dramatic.

M. had heard high fevers cause brain damage.

He didn't know if C. was allergic to Motrin®.

I don't know, M. said. How could he know?

Diarrhea, yes. No vomiting. Yes. Vomiting. Some.

The nurse stabbed a vein in C.'s foot, taped it, drew blood.

An ear infection, maybe a virus.

Then they could go home. They could follow up with Dr. S
———.

They couldn't do anything, really, except feel bad for C., and C., who woke from the crying.

M. scratched.[28]

---

[28] Triamcinolone, Diprolene®, Elidel®[1]

Q. What is eczema?

A. Eczema is a general term encompassing various inflamed skin conditions.

It spread across M.'s shoulders, then tapered to the base of his spine. He had a round welt between his belly button and rib cage, and in the webbing between his fingers and on his palms. When he smoked discount reds from the reservation, it spread to his fingernails, which dimpled like golf balls.[2]

It splotched C.'s face and neck, and his stomach and chest and legs, migrating in clumps. It was inflamed and moist and flaky, and it wept yellow Rorschachs onto his shirts.

People commented.

M. didn't know what to say.

[1] Topical corticosteroids treat skin conditions, such as eczema, psoriasis, insect bites, and hives.[1]

[1] Side Effects Cannot be Anticipated. But a possible side effect of Diprolene is stinging or burning of the skin where the medication is applied. Other side effects on the skin may include: Acne-like eruptions,[1] atrophy, "broken" capillaries (fine reddish lines), cracking or tightening, dryness, excess hair growth, infected hair follicles, inflammation, irritation, itching, prickly heat, rash, redness, sensitivity to touch.

[1] The acne, M. found out, was a permanent side effect, unless he tried Accutane®, which for him was a lousy bet.[1]

[1] Some patients, while taking Accutane or soon after stopping Accutane, have become depressed or developed other serious mental problems. Some people tried to end their own lives. And some people have ended their own lives. There were reports that some of these people did not appear depressed.[1]

[1] Center for Drug Evaluation and Research <http://www.fda.gov/cder/drug/infopage/accutane/medicationguide.htm>

[2] Eczema tends to be worse in smokers and is exacerbated by caffeine.

A. The causes of certain types of eczema remain to be explained, though atopic eczema is thought to be a hereditary condition, being genetically linked.

For M., the itching grew worse in evenings, when the kids were fed, and at loose ends, and C. scooted from living room to dining room to kitchen and back and again. M. used a back-scratcher, knowing he shouldn't,[1] and sawed until his skin burned.

M. numbed his hands under hot water.[2]

S. said nothing.

Before the kids, she had boils of acne that she picked until they ran clear fluid.

Pregnant, her skin cleared (though she couldn't stand the weight on her hips).

Puberty, M. knew, would make C.'s skin slick with grease, turning the rashes yeasty.

C. would hate him for it.[3]

C., M. said. Marathon man. Let's try to relax.

[1] Eczema is "the itch that rashes." Scratching intensifies the development of the rash.

[2] **A.** Run hot water—as hot as you can stand—over the affected area for 5 to 10 minutes. This seems counterintuitive, because it will increase the itching. But after a few minutes, the nervous circuits seem to get overloaded and the itching stops for a long time.[1]

[1] Ask Dr. Weil. <http://www.drweil.com/app/cda/drw_cda.html-command=TodayQA-questionId=3599>

[3] There are no guarantees that a child will grow out of eczema. However, research has shown that 60–70% of children are virtually clear of the condition by the time they reach their mid-teens.

A. The first step in effective treatment of eczema is a correct diagnosis.

Right, Dr. _____ said. He wore gabardine pants and a white coat. He rubbed a patch on C.'s leg.

He's in daycare, Dr. _____ said.

Right, M. said.

Ringworm, Dr. _____ said.

Ringworm, M. said.

The kids at daycare, Dr. _____ said. Contagious.

Like a dog, M. said.

Not exactly, Dr. ____ said. But, yes.

The doctor says it looks like ringworm, M. said.

And what do we do, S. said.

I don't know, M. said.

He said it's viral, M. said.

So nothing, S. said.

No, Dr. ****** said, touching a lesion on C.'s chest. It's a fungus.[1]

I thought it was viral, M. said.

Use Lamisil®, Dr. ****** said. She wore a white coat.

But not on that, she said. That's eczema.

That's eczema, M. asked.

That's eczema, she said.

Steroid cream, she said. Use it on the eczema, she said.

Not on the tinea, Dr. ****** said. It makes it worse,[2] she said. The tinea.

What, M. said.

What the fuck, M. said.

Fucking christ, M. said.

Motherfucker, M. said.

Knock it off, S. said.

[1] Ringworm is an infection of the skin caused by a fungus. Ringworm can affect your skin anywhere on your body (tinea corporis), your scalp (tinea capitis), your groin area (tinea cruris, also called jock itch), or feet (tinea pedis, also called athlete's foot).

Often, there are several patches of ringworm on your skin at once.

[2] Some ringworm infections, especially those treated with a steroid like hydrocortisone, can have vesicles or pustules in the advancing border or in the center.[1]

[1] ABOUT.COM. <http://dermatology.about.com/cs/fungalinfections/a/ringworm.htm>

A. Links with environmental factors and stress are being explored.

C. scratched in his sleep, pulling red welts like worms across his belly.

S. didn't cry when she saw them.

She clipped C.'s nails, and filed them, and thought about gloves.

They bleached blood from his sheets.

S. cried to M., who worried about what he didn't know.

A. Eczema is not contagious and, like many diseases, currently cannot be cured. <http://www.querycat.com/faq/03ec4229392c5b2297550f479e2 53220>

From the health food co-op, S. bought cream with Aloe Vera, Calendula, Jojoba, and Vitamins A, D, and E. She spread it behind C.'s knees before bed, and during the day, when M. asked C. to please not scratch.

It makes it worse, M. said.

Honey, M. said. Please.

, C. said.

I know, M. said.

It itches, M. said.

C., M. said. Stop it.

You stop it, S. said.

I wasn't yelling, M. said.

Honey, M. said. I wasn't yelling.

C. said, Stop.

C., M. said. I'm sorry.

Distract him, S. said.

You, M. said.

Honey, M. said. Let's go outside.

Okay, M. said.

Stop, C. said. STOP.

Honey, M. said. Okay.

It's okay, M. said.

S. kept the babies in her office, one, one year, and then the other,[29] the next, with help from Ali, from American lit, and Gina and Sarah, from the freshman seminar.

S. fed between classes, when she prepped, and graded, too.

The crying, when it happened, brought Hong Wu from religious studies, and James Newton, in English, from upstairs. Once, the dean of the college stopped by, curious. She wore black pants and a red blouse and a black blazer.

S. looked into and bought what they'd need:[30] eczema wash, baby Tylenol, nipple pads.

---

[29] and they went, one, and then the other, to daycare, at six months, when they grew stronger.

[30] Rubber nipples they boiled before use. The same with bottles, and bottle lids, and pacifiers.

They washed the rubber breast pump plugs. The breast pump had a battery pack and car-lighter adapter. The label told them to *Breast at Ease!* S. used it on days when supply exceeded demand, bottling, then freezing the excess.

They owned a crib, a changing table, two strollers, two baby buckets, two baby bucket bases—for the cars, two car seats, bibs, cloth diapers, disposable diapers, ointment, sheets, onesies, blankets, a swing.

Before C. could lift his head, they owned two shelves of baby books and three baskets of toys.

They had a cradle, a baby backpack, a BabyBjörn®, a Boppy® pillow, and two Boppy knockoffs. They owned a plastic bouncy car with center harness.

They owned a dozen Avent® bottles. C. preferred Gerber® bottles, so they bought those, too.

And.

People are generous, M. said.

Look at this stuff, M. said.

Babies are expensive, S. said.

She stayed up nights, feeding.

She bought and borrowed and adjusted clothes to fit her shrinking body.

She did laundry. She washed dishes. The dog. She walked the dog.

S. took the kids to the pediatrician.

She took naps, infrequently.

She cried into a blanket when her parents' visit ended, and they stood at the door.

Why couldn't they stay a little longer?

She was tired.

S. resented exhaustion.

She hated the neighborhood, the noise, and their house, which was too damn small.

Her students didn't pay attention.

People like buying, he thought.

S.'s mother shared a website that offered catalogues, from companies of all kinds.

It made him angry, that C. was an excuse to go shopping.

He was grateful to have the stuff.

The shopping cart had bad wheels, and the city smelled. Bad drivers. Bad coffee.

What kind of idiots call after eight?

S. called M. selfish. Self-involved. Asshole.

S. couldn't be mad at the babies.

M. felt tired, too.[31]

He mowed the lawn during naps.˙If S. went out, he mowed one-handed, the other pressing a baby monitor against his ear.

He left his coffee on a fencepost, drinking as he passed.

Addie, next door, watched from her deck. Sometimes she'd wave, and laugh.

---

[31] What, he said. What?

What, she said.

Fuck, he said, fuck.

What, she said. Stop it.

God, no, he said. Oh, God.

What, she said, stop it.

Fucking shut up, he said, shut up.

You shut up she said, stop it.

What's her problem, he said. Go feed her.

I did, she said. She's teething.

Fuck, he said. No.

Stop it, she said. Get up.

No, he said. Fuck you.[1]

[1] "Not getting enough sleep impairs our work performance, increases the risk for injuries and makes it more difficult to get along with others," says Mark Rosekind, Ph.D., an expert on fatigue and performance issues. "Without sufficient sleep it is more difficult to concentrate, make careful decisions and follow instructions, we are more likely to make mistakes or errors, and are more prone to being impatient and lethargic."[1]

[1] The National Sleep Foundation. "Stress, Anxiety, and Sleep."
<http://sleepdisorders.about.com/cs/stressandanxiety/a/nsfanxiety.htm>

Zantac®

Greasy lunches burned a hole in M.'s esophagus. His leg and knee ached from pressing the clutch.

His favorite green shirt showed a vomit stain. He wore it anyway.

His back ached from twisting his hips out, to bob C., or from hunching sideways to hold a toy, spinning, over C.'s nose.

Sometimes he behaved like a prick.[32]

---

[32] At one time or another:

M. pretended he didn't hear the baby cry,

used excuses to stay away from home,

blamed his lateness on long lines, or on traffic.

He complained about what they did on weekends.

He didn't suggest alternatives.

He walked ahead at the zoo.

He got mad about spilt milk.

He called the baby names. He apologized. He did it again.

He thought about fucking women at work.

He didn't give a shit, sometimes, about what S. needed.

He did a lousy job on the dishes.

He jerked the dog's leash.

He cut people off in traffic.

He told panhandlers to get a job.

He badmouthed S.'s family.[1]

[1]Depression may complicate this picture. While 89% of mothers have symptoms of post-partum depression, 62% of fathers also showed depressive symptoms (Wetzsteon, 1983).

Sometimes he wedged lists onto scraps of paper and envelope backs.

MONDAY

M.
Dressed babies (a.m.)
Changed babies (3 times)
Straightened living room
Emptied dishwasher
Got gas in grey car
Walked dog (p.m.)
Made dinner
Dishes in dishwasher

S.
Made coffee (a.m.)
One load of laundry
Fed babies (all)
Walked dog (a.m.)

TUESDAY

M.
Dressed babies (a.m.)
Changed babies (3 times)
Walked dog (a.m. & p.m.)
Dishes in dishwasher
Drugstore
Grocery store
Gave babies a bath

S.
Made coffee (a.m.)
Paid bills
Made frozen pizza
Boiled nipples and bottles
Changed babies (1)

He just wanted to know: Who did more?

Petty man.

The common thread that runs throughout all of these transitions is the experience of grief. At a time our culture defines as joyous, it would seem selfish for the new father to acknowledge and express his personal griefs. The very people the new father might seek out to hear his pain may be those who are counting on him to be "strong," which implies silently supporting the new family financially. New fathers may feel vulnerable, alone, or act out to avoid these feelings entirely.[1]

[1] Mergler, Randy and Roger Coughlan. "New Fathers: Transitions and Griefs."
<http://www.lapas.org/merghlan96.html>

He stared at women. Laura, in her cinch-top nurse pants. Jamie, inscrutable. Anna. And Jackie, her breasts shifting under a loose blouse. Ellen, thin, pigtailed, her pants snug. Sarah, with tight t-shirts and red converse sneakers. Lydia, who watched him back.

He surfed the internet. He jerked off.

<http://www.girlsongirlsyum.com/herfirstlesbiansex/big olestrapon.html>

He whined to his brother. He said that his friends without kids were like kids.

They had time to themselves.

They didn't have to schedule their days to the hour.

They didn't always have dishes to do. Or laundry. Or work around the house.

They didn't miss the news, then miss the news, then miss the news, and then ask, what happened?

They didn't talk about poopies, and peepies, and burping.

They didn't feel so put upon.

They didn't sound like their parents.

Zoloft®

S. stopped breastfeeding and asked her doctor for Zoloft.[33]

She suggested M. do the same, because he worried.

About what did he worry.

---

[33] HOW ZOLOFT WORKS

<http://www.zoloft.com/zoloft/zoloft.portal?_nfpb=true&_pageLabel=how_zoloft_works>

Zoloft® (sertraline HCl) is a type of antidepressant known as a selective serotonin reuptake inhibitor or SSRI.

Nerve cells in the brain and the rest of the nervous system use chemical messengers. These messengers help cells send messages to each other. One of these messengers is called serotonin.

Studies show that serotonin plays a vital role in how our body works. It controls sleep, appetite, temperature, and blood vessel tone. It's also in charge of the release of certain hormones and how much pain we feel.

Because it is linked with so many functions in our body, serotonin has an effect on a wide range of conditions such as depression.

This tie between depression and serotonin led scientists to an interesting find. Scientists believe people with depression could have an imbalance of serotonin in their brain.

M. worried that his taglines for the Christian colleges didn't have sparkle, and sincerity, and verve!

Put faith in your education!

He worried about Clovis, in the next office, with her tummy rolls, and loose arms, because she wanted attention, and he didn't have any to give. He worried Clovis might lose him his job, and he had babies to support, and the house, and his wife, and the rest of his life, ruined.

He worried Clovis would let him keep his job, and he'd float by, and hate it, and spend his life sucking up.

He worried he'd hate his kids for it.

That means the level of serotonin is "off." So the nerve cells can't communicate, or send messages to each other the right way. This lack of contact between cells might cause depression.

Zoloft helps fix this. Zoloft helps the nerve cells send messages to each other the way they normally should.

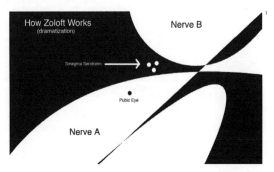

[1] *Depression, an Illness that Can Be Treated,* published by Pfizer Company®, the manufacturer of Zoloft. Image by Mark Yakich.

He worried he'd hate S. for convincing him to work for the money, and the insurance, and the long term, and a house, and a minivan.

He worried he'd start believing in getting by, becoming a distant, tired, quiet relative of himself.

He worried he'd never stop worrying.

Paxil®

He worried
about C.

The crying.

C.'s rash.

About Sue,
at work.

His project.

Cuts.

M. had heard
of Paxil. He
said Paxil to Dr.
_____, who
asked what dose.

I don't know,
M. said. Maybe
half. Ten mil-
ligrams, M. said,
five, and tried,
and went back.

It's better, he said,
so ten, he said,
started, and his
stomach spun.

Tea.

No coffee.

Their savings.

He checked
his zipper.

And John, in
the hall.

That look.

The roof.

Flashing.

The board on
the porch.

Blades.

Locks.

Streets.

He worried
about the dog.

Disease.

Cleaning fluids.

The gas in
the garage.

Dry mouth.

His stool turned
loose, and M. said,
Wrong. His arms
shook. He said to
S., This is wrong.

They go away,
S. said. She said,
Don't stop.

You can't start
and stop and start
and stop, she said.

Loose.

Stool.

He didn't fin-
ish his soup.

Dizzy, he held
tables. No one
noticed.

The belching.

It stopped.

Maybe S., he
thought.

Or C.

Mint.

Milk.

Sugar.

If he wants.

Or S.

Decaf.

The freezer.

S.

Decaf.

C.

.

Tea.

Black.

Milk.

The back stairs.

S. falling.

Steve didn't
say hello.

Had he said.

The older kids.

Too rough.

He'd stared.

S. would yell.

He wasn't do-
ing his share.

The phone bill.

Dad's meds.

And Mom.

Her ankles.

And C.

Diapers.

Daycare.

All of it.

A firm shit.

Fine.

Good.

Surprise.

Fine, he said to S.

To Dr. _____,
M. said, Twenty.

I'll halve them, he
said, the copay,
and he did, and
then he didn't,
and he felt sick
on the way up.
Then he slept.

He went to bed
just after C.

He needed
his sleep.

C. still cries at
night, S. said.

Sugar.

Not boiled.

The big cup.

Earl Grey.

Or soda.

Water.

Brita.

The fridge.

S.'s bottle.

Juice.

For C.

He had to pee.

Juice.

C.

Water.

For S.

Right.

Runny noses.

The two of them.

Their friends.

And the car.

Probably.

The plumbing.

Or furnace.

He was weak.

Uninvolved.

S. said.

Self-involved.

Boring.

Typical.

Ron, at work.

That look.

What.

If he hadn't
noticed.

He yawned driv-
ing to work.

During meet-
ings, into his lap.

He listened to
Clovis, and Sue
and Ron. He
missed sentences,
he thought. It
didn't matter.

He got the gist.

Whatever.

His ankle, jogging,
it didn't hurt.

The sleep.

He mowed the
lawn. He took
out the garbage.
Cleaned the
garage. Emptied
the gutters.

C. helped him.

What.

What.

They planted
shrubs.

What got done.

S. was tired.

You want to,
he said.

Are you kid-
ding, she said.

Okay, he said.

Was he stupid?

Not stupid, M. thought.

A large pie, he said. No sauce.

Tomatoes and onions.

Wait, he said, shouldering the phone. Okay?

No, S. said. I want sauce.

I'm sorry, he said. Can we start over?

Like that, he thought. Thoughtless.

I wasn't thinking, he said. I'm sorry.

I don't like that, she said.

I know, he said.

I'm busy.

And C. And C.

The medicine, he thought.

It's the point.

To not notice.

What, he said.

I asked, S. said, what will the kids eat.

I don't know, M. said. Pizza, he said. And peaches.

I'll get the peaches, he said. And juice.

Milk, S. said.

Okay, he said. Milk.

A liability.

You miss stuff, he thought.

Yes, honey, he said. Pizza.

Pizza, C. said. Za. Za.

Shit, usually.

The worrying.

It's not normal, he thought. Worrying.[34]

Wjoe the mouye for the dededebay, S. said.

I'm sorry, M. said. What.

Money, she said. For the pizza.

Yeah, he said. No. I mean, I'll write a check.

They take checks, he said.

---

[34] For a while, ideas passed into checking, and M. ran a finger up his zipped zipper, pushing the pulltab to his pants button. He did it inside, outside. He couldn't stop. People noticed. The embarrassment made him want to check again, which he did, pretending to straighten his buckle.

He checked zippers on jackets backpacks bags purses (S.'s), running his finger along the closed teeth until hitting a pull, and doing it again.[1]

He checked doorknob locks, deadbolts, drawer locks, and car locks.

And again.

If he could have, he would have washed and washed his hands, but they were raw with eczema that covered his stomach and back.

[1] Compulsions are acts the person performs over and over again, often according to certain "rules." People with an obsession about contamination may wash constantly to the point that their hands become raw and inflamed. A person may repeatedly check that she has turned off the stove or iron because of an obsessive fear of burning the house down. She may have to count certain objects over and over because of an obsession about losing them.[1]

[1] Obsessive-Compulsive Foundation. "What is OCD." <http://www.ocfoundation.org/ocf1010a.htm>

I don't know, S. said.

Okay, he said.

Age, he thought. Your memory.

It goes.

It's never one thing, he thought.

Brownies.

Brownies for dessert, M. said. Brownies, C.

She helped make them, S. said.

Brownies, C. said.

Nice, S. said. Make a big deal before dinner.

Well they know, M. said, if she helped.

You're cheerful, he thought.

Take people on their terms.

It's what you have to do, he thought. To get along.

You want water, he said. Or soda.

I don't care, she said. Water.

Get out of your rut. Stubbornness.

But the vagueness, he thought.

No focus.

Everything comes in around the edges, he thought.

And goes out like that.

You need to clench to focus, he thought.
Your nervous system clenches.

No wonder I can't come,[35] he thought.

You ready, M. said. A few more minutes.

Library tonight, S. said.

---

[35] Instead of raising libido and the ability to achieve sexual fulfillment, popular antidepressants commonly cause a loss of interest in sex and block the ability to achieve sexual satisfaction.... Drug-related problems, which occur in women as often as in men, may include decreased or lost libido; inability to achieve an erection or ejaculation; and delayed or blocked orgasm.[1] [2]

[1] No, M. said. If I get interested, he said, I can.

?

You know.

Function, Eric said.

Yeah, M. said, function.

So, Eric said, get interested.

Okay, said M., but then I can't, you know.

?

.

.

Have an orgasm.

I'm tractable, he thought.

Okay, he said.

Which she likes.

There's a candy bar, M. thought.

Less aggravating.

Never, said Eric.

Not never, M. said, but not for, like, an hour.

Wow, Eric said. Sign me up.

For Paxil, Eric said.

It's awful, M. said, exhausting.

Yeah, Eric said, I guess. But S. doesn't complain.

M. said, Well.

What, Eric said.

Don't say it, Eric said.

She gets sore, M. said.

Man, Eric said.

Yeah, M. said.

Is it impotence, Eric said, or is that just, you know, limpness?

I think it's erectile dysfunction, M. said.

I kinda always figured it was the same with guys taking Viagra®, Eric said. No payoff.

I don't know, M. said.

Like after prostate surgery, Eric said. There's stuff missing.

My dad's friend had it, Eric said. A real bummer, he said. The guy was a swordsman in his youth.

A swordsman, M. said.

It's what my dad said, Eric said. Fucked up, huh?

What, M. said.

Right.

Brownies.

A little stupid, he thought.

And the sweating,[36] he thought.

It's where your body worries you know.

What, he said.

That he used the word swordsman, Eric said.

Yeah, M. said.

He shows people pictures of his scar, Eric said.

His scar, M. said.

His friend, Eric said, where they cut it out.

I think just guys, Eric said.

He thinks it's funny, Eric said.

It is kind of funny, M. said.

Yeah, Eric said.

But not that funny, M. said.

[2] Brody, Jane E. "Personal Health: Antidepressants and Libido." *The New York Times on the Web.*
<http://depression.about.com/gi/dynamic/offsite.htm?site=http%3A%2F%2Fwww.ny-times.com%2Fspecials%2Fwomen%2Fwarchive%2F960515_1126.html >

[36] The most common side effects of SSRIs include nausea, sweating, fatigue, and sleepiness.[1] [2]

[1] At night, M.'s eyes closed watching TV, or reading, or talking on the phone.

Lisa stayed late visiting, lonely after Scott left. M. fell asleep on the floor.

He yawned through meetings, and meals. He sat quietly if he could.

How little life requires motivation, or much thought. He found he didn't miss them.

He had less to say, which was best.

[2] <http://www.paxil.com/depression/dp_pxl.html#question4>

E.[37] & L.[38]

E. cut her dose from twenty milligrams to ten, then five.

Still she got zaps[39] that ran from her heel to her tailbone, up her elbow to her armpit, and alongside her spine. Turning her head made them flit across her shoulders.

Like a whack on the funny bone, she said to L.

She had nausea, at night, when she lay down and had to stretch her arms to still the bed.[40] She got up at six, when the turning of her stomach grew urgent, and bumped walls to the toilet, which she spattered with loose stool.

She would scrub the bowl, but only after a piece of toast and coffee and starting the laundry and straightening the kitchen.

Her brain took time to understand what her fingers touched or her eyes saw.

---

[37] Enrollee

[38] Legal Guardian

[39] **What are "The Zaps"?** The zaps are little shock-like sensations, which occur during Paxil withdrawal. They can happen with head and eye movement, or even while sitting perfectly still. After a while, you can begin to hear the zaps happening in your head—like a 'swoosh' sound. <http://paxil.bizland.com/jbuzzw.htm>

[40] Patients who stop taking Paxil abruptly often experience dizziness, nausea, diarrhea, and vertigo. Therefore, slow tapering is recommended. <http://www.nami.org/Template.cfm?Section=About_Medications&template=/ContentManagement/ContentDisplay.cfm&ContentID=7394>

She said, I'm off kilter.

It's hard to explain, she said.

I don't want to be on it forever, she told Dr. XXXXXXX, who agreed, but said

> If intolerable symptoms occur following a decrease
> in the dose or upon discontinuation of treatment,
> then resuming the previously prescribed dose may be
> considered (see DOSAGE AND ADMINISTRATION).

Keep me posted, he said.

I don't want to take it forever, E. said to L.,

Why stop, L. said. If it helps.

E. opened her mouth. She took 40 mg of-Lipitor® to lower her cholesterol. She took Xanax before meetings. She took Advil® for cramps and Tylenol for headaches. She carried Prevacid® in her purse—in case of red sauce. She took the pill because Greg couldn't come in a rubber, and Claritin® in ragweed months.

I'm thirty-seven, E. said.

I'm better, she said.

who turned to watch a boy pause, and bend, and tie his shoe. L. thought the boy was nineteen or twenty. He was too thin. He walked to the counter to order a Mocha Valencia. L. liked the hoops that ran one two three four five up his earlobe. She thought she saw two more outlined in the fabric of his shirt, at his nipples. She touched her hand to her nose and imagined sour sheets. She wanted to tease him. Who orders a Mocha Valencia.

The long-term side effects,[41] she said.

I take too many pills, E. said.

Oh, L. said. | She took too many pills, too. But she got up three, four times a night to comfort C.[1] and C.[2]

[1] Child
[2] Child

She couldn't walk to the bathroom without kicking piles of laundry. She hadn't been to a movie in two years. She needed Zoloft®. Without Zoloft, she'd stab R.[1] to death.[2]

[1] Relation, who took Paxil and couldn't hold more than two things in his mind at a time[1] and left details of family life to L., as if she wore curlers and spent days home folding laundry and cooking roast beef. She didn't. She worked. They were vegetarian.

[1] What are the possible side effects of Paxil?
Nervous System: Central Nervous System stimulation, concentration impaired. <http://www.onlinelawyersource.com/paxil/faq.html>

[2] SUBJECT: ZOLOFT AND LACK OF FEELINGS TOPIC AREA: DEPRESSION
Question Posted By: kristine on Sunday, June 18, 2000.
I have been taking 50 mg. of Zoloft for two years now to treat mild depression and social anxiety. Since I've been taking Zoloft, I don't seem to "feel" my feelings anymore. Like anger. Or if I'm experiencing a sad situation, it registers that "I am sad" or "this is sad," but I don't feel the actual sadness that I used to prior to Zoloft. In fact, I can't even cry (and I used to enjoy a good cry now and then). Is this normal for Zoloft? <http://www.medhelp.org/forums/mentalhealth/messages/31088a.html>

[41] It must be conceded that we do not yet know the long-term effects of Paxil or related agents (called SSRIs, and include Prozac® and Zoloft), if by long-term, you mean, "after 10 or more years of use." These agents are still too "new" to generate that kind of data. <http://www.mhsource.com/expert/exp1081996a.html>

Effects, L. said.

.

.

Well, E. said.

E. didn't want to forget she liked the newspaper, and that she liked chili with jalapeños and talking to her sister on the phone at night.[42] She enjoyed sex once.[43]

It changes you, she said.

---

[42] After only a little of the *Times* on Sunday, E. lost focus and started thinking of mowing the lawn, and she didn't like kidney beans anymore. She couldn't ever, ever stay up past ten.[1]

> [1] Continue to take paroxetine and talk to your doctor if you experience
> - impaired concentration;
> - changes in appetite or weight;
> - sleepiness or insomnia; or
> - decreased sex drive, impotence, or difficulty having an orgasm.
> Side effects other than those listed here may also occur. <http://paxil.drugs.com/>

[43] but lately her clitoris had less feeling than a pinky toe.

Body System/Adverse Event	% Reporting Event	
	PAXIL CR (n = 212)	Placebo (n = 211)
Female Genital Disorder[8,11]	10%	<1%
Impotence[9]	5%	3%
Urinary Tract Infection	3%	1%
Menstrual Disorder[9]	2%	<1%
Vaginitis[9]	2%	0%

1. Adverse events for which the PAXIL CR reporting incidence was less than or equal to the placebo incidence are not included. These events are: Abnormal dreams, anxiety, arthralgia, depersonalization, dysmenorrhea, dyspepsia, hyperkinesia, increased appetite, myalgia, nervousness, pharyngitis, purpura, rash, respiratory disorder, sinusitis, urinary frequency, and weight gain.
2. <1% means greater than zero and less than 1%.
3. Mostly flu.
4. A wide variety of injuries with no obvious pattern.
5. Pain in a variety of locations with no obvious pattern.
6. Most frequently seasonal allergic symptoms.
7. Usually flushing.
8. Mostly blurred vision.
9. Based on the number of males or females.
10. Mostly anorgasmia or delayed ejaculation.
11. Mostly anorgasmia or delayed orgasm.

<http://us.gsk.com/products/assets/us_paxilcr.pdf>

What doesn't, L. said, | thinking of shrimp sopped in butter.

Nights, she crammed dinner in her mouth faster than she could chew. She snitched macaroni from C.'s plate. She longed for a cigarette.

I wasn't always fat as a house, L. said.

You're not, said E.

Kids change us, L. said. Age changes us. Jobs. Friends.

I know, E. said.

But those are real, E. said. I don't know, she said, stirring her coffee, which was skin-colored and cold. It's your brain,[44] she said.

Your brain, L. said. | Her brain ruined her, even at 100 mg a day.

She thought of C.'s narrow shoulder blades and the fine down of hair on his back. She saw him laughing as he splashed his feet in the tub. In fifteen years, he would have earrings and long, dirty hair, and the back pocket of his jeans would fray from the wear of his wallet. He would be thin and spend mornings in a bed with sour sheets. Her son.

---

[44] A psychoactive drug or psychotropic substance is a chemical that alters brain function, resulting in temporary changes in perception, mood, consciousness, or behavior. Extreme use can have permanent affects on the brain. **Stimulants** Cocaine Amphetamine Caffeine Nicotine **Psychedelics** LSD Mescaline Psilocybin Cannabis PCP MDMA ("Ecstasy") DMT

I'm thinking of actually increasing my dose, L. said.

I'm depressed,[45] L. said.

| Too busy to wipe his ass. |

Maybe I'll go up to 150, she said. I'm not going down. | She wasn't trying to be mean. |

That's me, she said. Not you.

I'm depressed, she said again, and she laughed. E. did too.

That wasn't it, E. said. For me.

E. said, It was worrying.

I couldn't stop,[46] she said, before Paxil, she said, which made her sweat from her palms and her feet and even her tongue.

Ketamine Salvinorin A **Narcotics** Opiates Morphine Codeine Heroin **Sedatives** Ethyl alcohol Benzodiazepines Valium GHB **Anti-depressants** SSRIs Prozac Zoloft Paxil **Antipsychotics** Haloperidol (Haldol) **Aphrodisiacs** PT-141 <http://en.wikipedia.org/wiki/Psychotropic_drug>

[45] Like L., R. had put on weight, since the kids, but in his torso. His breasts hung. His bellybutton had sunk to a crater, and he could stick a finger in to the second knuckle, which he did. He was meaty. He had to adjust his gut to enter her. Sex felt like rolling around in sweaters.

His underwear had taken on new stains. L. suspected he wasn't wiping.

[46] BP,[1] everything linked. The meeting she missed meant John's look and William calling her in about what wasn't clear, but he was mad, and her job meant benefits, and she couldn't start looking for work again. She had house payments, and she wouldn't count on U.[2] She took care of herself, and her sister, too, in most ways, which was fine, but she worried, and she should have let it all go, every time, but she didn't, and she wound tighter till her back ached and her hands shook, and she replayed events, thinking them over and over and over and over. She repeated sentences after she said them. To make

Her arms shook. But she waded through the side effects, and they went away.

Then she relaxed. She could take a deep breath.

She slept ten hours a night. She smiled at William, at work, when he boiled up. She felt compassion for his position.

She stopped worrying about the traffic downtown.

She didn't care that her clutch was starting to go, or about gas prices.

She didn't care that she sat all day.

---

sure they'd come out right. To make sure they had come out right. To make sure they sounded right. People noticed. Who wouldn't notice, and E. felt less confident, and it showed in her work, and her posture, which was rigid and hunched, her elbows glued to her sides. She stared at people, trying to see what they really meant, and it made them nervous, which made her nervous, and powerless to change. Impotent. She asked her primary health provider about meds, and he said

> The effectiveness of PAXIL in the treatment of Generalized Anxiety Disorder (GAD) was demonstrated in two 8-week, multicenter, placebo-controlled studies (Studies 1 and 2) of adult outpatients with Generalized Anxiety Disorder (DSM-IV).
> <http://www.healthyplace.com/medications/paroxetine.asp>

What dose,[3] he said.

She knew she should see a therapist, too, but she didn't.

[1] Before Paxil.

[2] Unrelated

[3] "It is easier to get a prescription refilled than approval for therapy. The insurance industry will not be moved, and clients think a pill is best." Dr. Gary R. Sweeten <http://www.talkingcure.com/archive/drugs.htm>

She didn't care if she had the right shoes.

She didn't care if people noticed.

She didn't care to scrub her toilet.

She didn't care if her evening work got done, if U. had something else to do on Friday, or if her weekends were planned.

She didn't care about the neighbors' parties.

She just didn't.[47]

But I don't, she said. Not now. I know how to not worry.

As much as I can, she said. I mean not worry.

---

[47] JUNE 07, 2004   THREE CHEERS FOR APATHY

Paxil was the first of two drugs I was on for depression. While I didn't have suicidal thoughts on it, I like to refer to it as the apathy drug. You can continue to leave the house, go to work, etc. because you just don't care. In an extreme way. So extreme that it's really not hard for me to image some people taking the next step and thinking hey, why bother staying alive at all?[1] Oh, and this probably won't surprise you, but GlaxoSmithKline®, maker of Paxil, loves Republicans. And why not? It worked well for Enron® and, to a lesser extent, Worldcom®.

Posted by morgaana on June 7, 2004 05:58 AM | TrackBack
<http://abracapocus.org/archives/002671.html>

[1] F.D.A. Toughens Warning on Antidepressant Drugs
By GARDINER HARRIS

Published: October 16, 2004

Heeding the recommendation of an advisory committee, the Food and Drug Administration ordered pharmaceutical companies yesterday to add strong warnings to antidepressants, saying the drugs could cause suicidal thoughts and actions in some children and teenagers.
<http://www.nytimes.com/2004/10/16/politics/16depress.html?adxnnl=1&adxnnlx=1098111690->

So why not stop, she said.

Sure, L. said, though she didn't mean it, which E. knew, because she wasn't stupid.

E. was tired.

She wanted coffee, and she wanted to talk to L., who didn't pay attention but talked about her kids and her kids and her kids, like she was the first fucking parent in the world.

E. listened every time and said, I know it's hard.

Too much for L.

Too much that E. asked for anything.

Please.

L. at the center of the room, fat bitch.

Blah blah me me blah blah blah me me me blah.

Cunt.

E. thought about smashing L.'s face down on the cups and plates until her teeth cracked and her cheeks crumpled around her nose.

She put her hands on her legs.

Maybe I'm feeling irritable,[48] she said.

Oh, honey, L. said.

---

[48] **Think you might be experiencing Paxil withdrawal?**

Take this simple test. Are you:

• Scared?
• Confused?
• Sick?
• Tired?
• And very, very angry??!
• You must be trying to discontinue paxil![1] <http://join-the-fun.com/paxil-withdrawal.html>

[1] Paxil Withdrawal
According to World Health Organization ("WHO"), "Paxil has the highest incidence rate of withdrawal adverse experiences of any antidepressant drug in the world." Symptoms include severe mood swings, like extreme irritability and anger.[1] <http://www.anattorneyforyou.com/legal/px_topics130.htm>

[1] SUBJECT: PAXIL WITHDRAWAL (SEVERE) AND ANY HELPFUL MEDICATION
TOPIC AREA: ANXIETY   FORUM: THE MENTAL HEALTH FORUM
Question Posted By: pharmno062 on Sunday, May 16, 2004

My husband has been withdrawing from Paxil for two plus weeks now and is experiencing: disorientation, confusion, anger outbursts. He cannot sleep with regularity and rants and raves non-stop. He has a good psychiatrist and is on neurontin and is not diagnosed with any other severe DSM-IV diagnostic disorder. He is trying small amounts of xanax and very small dosages of vicodin, which gives him relief for 3 hours at a time. He does not want to take more drugs to complicate this situation or become addicted. He is not taking these medications in large dosages and has only been taking them for a week. Even this does not allow him to go out in public and function without going into confusion, a rage, or nearly have drastic automobile accidents. He also becomes combative at times.

Lithium

The thing about Eastern, it has daycare, which doesn't cost much, so I.[49] can swing it another year, till kindergarten. She will swing it, with money from dad. When he can spare it, he gives.

It's like this:

I. gets up with S.[50] and makes the beds. Showers, maybe, and wraps her hair and washes S.'s toes and her hands and her face. Drives to campus along Franklin to Main to Arbor to Elm to the center, where she says goodbye, it's just a while, and she kisses S. and produces a ratty bill and three quarters and some dimes to pay for S.'s lunch. Then to class, where she sits in a chair by the window and drinks from a green water bottle and takes notes and looks at the textures of people's skin. Later, she'll eat salad for lunch. And then more class, and then, for a work-study wage, two hours copying articles, cutting her fingers on the pages and leaving xeroxed thumbprints. With the copier lid up, the room strobes—and the heat, such a small room, full of ozone and burning toner. Then she'll get S.

The smell of floor polish in the library halls.

Flowery detergent coming off the clothes of kids in classrooms.

---

[49] Injured

[50] Same Last Name, First Name, Middle Initial

College bathrooms ripe with the smell of radiators and shit.

I. has to think ahead. She has to go to the store. She has to get S. to Grams on Saturday and on Sunday, so she can study. She has to find time over Thanksgiving. She has to keep her GPA. She has to keep her aid. She has to graduate, with honors, because she wants an M.L.S. and to find a job in a city of a half-million people. She has to rent a loft apartment. She has to get a cat. She has to have a tub. She has to own a small microwave. She has to be able to walk S. to school and use public transportation. She has to wear pants to work. She has to read at least a book a week for the rest of her life.

She has to avoid thinking of things she can't do.

She has to own her thoughts.

She has to be nice.

She has to has to has to smoke outside, because she and S. can't lose their place.

She has to get some sleep.

In class, the girl with the low-cut shirt says she doesn't have a pen. Sorry, she says. She turns to the front of the room.

A boy in a polo shirt looks down when I. says she's got a kid.

At the union, she sits at her own table. Across the room, a boy with freckles shakes his salad bowl, to spread the dressing.

And they think I'm strange, I. thinks, and imagines sadness coming off her like a stink. She makes origami figures from gum wrappers and sets them afloat in a small fountain by the front hall, and the boys walk past in hoodies and goatees, the little thugs, and the girls in sweats with PINK on the ass.

I. thinks PINK means pussy.

She's only maybe five, six years older than these kids.

And there's never time, even if she leaves S. late and spends spare seconds in the library, in the cushioned chair across from the elevator, using highlighters to mark passages in her books and watching the elevator doors open and close and people get on and off.

She goes to every class and takes a back seat in the lecture halls and listens for news about assignments and exams.

I. says in her smaller class, she says that Updike seems dishonest. She asks why they aren't reading Acker. She says she likes books about upset women, or by upset women. Like Shelley Jackson. The professor asks, Who?

I. chews her pen caps to shreds. Then her fingernails.

She feels like shouting.

She says something mean to the girl who tries to talk to her after class.

She has acne across her cheeks and her chest.

She gets a case of Red Bull® from Sam's Club®.

She decides introductory classes don't teach you shit.

She plans her spring semester

PHL 225 FOUNDATION COGNITIVE TR 02:00P 03:15P
ENG 271 MODERN GRAMMAR MW 02:00P 03:15P
MST 550 MUSEUM COLLECT MGT/C W 06:00P 08:50P
ENG 323H FANTASY & SCI FICTIO TR 12:30P 01:45P
ENG 345 STUDIES IN AUTHORS MWF 01:00P 01:50P

and worries about the evening class and wonders if she can, maybe, get in the honors program and volunteer at the Women's Center and take kickboxing.

R.[51] says, That's a hell of a lot, which I. knows, she says, Thanks. Then she adds to the list, she adds,

I don't need your advice

which she hopes, she says, he'll keep in mind. Like.

He better know her apartment is her apartment. And when she wants to be alone, she wants to be alone. And dinner time is S.'s time, and so is after dinner time, and all night, and mornings, and all through the day. S.'s time. And what else? I. doesn't answer questions she doesn't like,[52] and she doesn't like gifts,

---

[51] Relationship to Injured?

[52] like about the past, because, truth of it, she once fucked a guy in a bathroom, at a party, and one guy she fucked in a car, on a folded back seat. One more and one more and one more in bedrooms with cheap posters, and one

and she doesn't share her shower, and she doesn't accept responsibility for birth control. She does her laundry and her daughter's, and that's fucking it.

Okay, R. says. R. says, I just want to help. I love you.

No, she says. She doesn't do love.

He should know that, too.

---

in the dirt, on the edges of a bonfire, before that guy called another one over.

She hitchhiked after stealing money from her mother's purse.

And missed half of high school.

Didn't sleep much at her mom's house or her dad's.

Had armpit hair and hair on her legs and walked at night, in her neighborhood.

She started conversations with strangers, just to see.

Stole books from the library.

Had online chats about sex. Arranged meetings with people and didn't show.

Wore men's suit trousers.

I. heard loud thoughts about how she brushed her teeth, and about how she walked, and about the things she said, and about what people said to her.

At seventeen, she smelled spring in January and stayed awake from Friday to Monday and came home with a bruised eye and an I shaved in her hair and picked at her scabs and talked about shiny sunglasses and clean countertops and apple skins.

She told her dad she'd wrecked his car.

It's out front, she said.

Wearing makeup makes me feel like a slut, she said.

Your stupid morality, she said.

I had a threesome.

I didn't use birth control.

I've got crabs.

I had a bucket on my head.

I'll only disappoint you.

You disappoint me, she said.

Tell me to fuck off.

I think I need a tampon.

It's not my period.

I'm a fucking joke.

Fuck you, I. said.

She said, Please don't hate me.

She left vomit stains on the toilet and slept during the day and lost weight and wanted to be dead because she would always be too stupid and too disgusting.

If her dad hadn't come home early, because.

How it felt when the fat EMT guy snaked a tube down her nose.

Seeing the night's food slide back through a clear plastic line.

They rinse you out with saline.

And arrest you.

And put you in a psych ward, where the metal doors crash shut.

Mesh covers the windows.

And patients smoke in the lounge.

Some wouldn't talk.

Some couldn't shut up.

She said to her dad it would make her worse, being there.

Her dad said,   .

.

.

When they released her, she had to see a counselor at the subsidized center, which had a psychiatrist on staff.

All psychiatrists keep candy in bowls.

It didn't help.

She doesn't like to answer questions about S.'s dad, because who?

And S.

For S. she started lithium, which gave her the shits, and cramps, and shaky hands, and it's why she always needs water and to watch her diet.

She'll never not take it.

And she'll not ever be pregnant again. Never risk not taking lithium.

So it's her and S., and that's just fine, and R. or whoever comes after can keep his fucking questions to himself.

S.[53] & P.[54] & C.[55] & C.[56]

Ginkgo Biloba

Morning

When the twins woke, S. put his hand on P., who rolled away.

S. swung from the bed. He walked to the bathroom.

Okay, he said, to C. and C. Okay.

He rinsed a plastic cup. He opened the medicine cabinet. He uncapped the B-100 supplements. Multivitamins. Ginkgo Biloba, and Gotu Kola. Garlic pills.

S. tapped them out. He put a handful in his mouth and threw his head back. He made a face and thought about brushing his teeth and heard P. walk down the hall. I have to pee, S. said,

---

[53] Subscriber

[54] Primary Subscriber

[55] Child

[56] Child

then followed P., and they got the girls diapered and dressed and downstairs and through breakfast.[57]

When Kitty came, P. left for the office. S. went to the kitchen and put on water and rinsed the teapot and said he'd go downstairs in five minutes. Five minutes, he said.

C. tied her fingers into his pants.

---

[57] And this is what he felt:

Multi-vitamin	B-100	Ginkgo Biloba	Gotu Kola	Garlic
Nothing. S. took it for the long term.	A flush of heat from the Niacin (which causes a rapid dilation of the small blood vessels (which feels like a hot flash (which S. knew because he owned three of Dr. Andrew Weil's books on natural health))).	Clearer thoughts.[1] [1] Ginkgo biloba is one of the most well researched herbs in the world, is full of anti-oxidants and flavonoids,[1] and supports healthy circulation to both the brain and extremities of the body. Studies suggest that this traditional Chinese remedy improves mental sharpness, concentration, and memory. [1] Flavonoids….	A kick in the ass, though no jitters.	S. had googled too many studies to think garlic lowered cholesterol or boosted immunity, but, still, he took it. P. said it made him smell. So did the vitamins. He smelled sour and yeasty, and he said sorry.

I know, he said, to C. Just till lunch. You play with Kitty, he said. Daddy's got work, S. said, but C. cried, and then C., too.

All right, then, he said and took a cup in one hand and the tea-pot in the other and shut the basement door with his foot.

Downstairs,[58] S. drank yerba maté (coffee gave him acid reflux).[59] He thought yerba maté tasted like tree bark. It had caffeine. It promised to:

· **Energize the Body**
· **Stimulate Mental Alertness**
· **Aid Weight Loss**
· **Cleanse the Colon**
· **Accelerate the Healing Process**
· **Relieve Stress**
· **Calm Allergies**
· **Fortify the Immune System**
· **Increase Longevity**

C. and C. would need him for twenty years, maybe more.

Years of diapers and baths and bedtime books, and then he'd shuttle soccer players or swimmers, and then music classes, and slumber parties, and then they'd have twin teenagers in the house, and, about that, S. expected the worst.

---

[58] S. and P.'s basement didn't sink below ground but sat on the ground floor, which their realtor called the garden level. P. said, It's a basement, because she wanted a lower price, which she got.

[59] ...for which, for a while, he took Prevacid®, because he couldn't give up his press-pot and espresso-maker and frothing pitcher and thermometer and demitasse cups and spoons and tamper. Now he stored them and, for P., put beans in the freezer, for her morning cup.

S. would be cooking and cleaning and buying groceries, because P. would always work sixty or seventy hours a week.

They'd stay in Atlanta, the girls in good schools, and they'd
always have more money than most.

He'd be a full-time dad until retirement, when he and P. could
travel, maybe, or buy condos in Aspen and New York.

But who's just a dad, S. wondered, and so stayed a grad student,
and used the hours before lunch to do what dissertators do:

1. He locked his office door and turned on his iMac and
   jerked off. He liked clips of Latin women bent over, or
   on their knees.

2. He visited Adagio Teas, at <http://www.adagio.com/>,
   and browsed and placed an order for eight ounces of
   lapsang souchong.

3. He called the Volvo® dealership about the wagon, which
   needed new brakes.

4. He replied to emails.

5. He checked bank statements, online, and transferred
   money to savings.

6. He listened to the girls' feet overhead, and Kitty's, and the
   sound of sweaters going on and the front door opening
   and closing.

7. He called the cleaning woman to cancel their week of vacation.

8. He drank a second and then third cup of tea and went upstairs for more, and to pee.

9. He called P. and left a voicemail about nothing, because she liked to hear his voice. He called about dinner reservations for Saturday, because Kitty could sit.

10. He looked into wireless stereo speakers and a furnace/ a/c unit for the attic.

11. He checked the clock and saw lunch coming and sent an interlibrary loan request for a new article. He read and took notes on another piece, which he'd photocopied. He looked back through the pages he'd written a week before, and changed some phrases. He added six sentences.

12. He heard Kitty come back with the girls, who shouted for him.

Lunch, he yelled, on his way up.

Lunch, he said, opening the basement door.

La, C. yelled back.

Afternoon

Naps stretched from one to four, after Kitty left.

The girls upstairs, S. filled the dishwasher and put away toys. He folded an afghan. He put boots in the closet. The vacuuming he left for the cleaning service. Ditto the mopping and the bathrooms.

Before they fell asleep, C. and C. shouted, for him, most, so S. set the baby monitor low and hoped they wouldn't crawl out of their cribs. He turned the TV to CNN and put music on the stereo. He made a pot of black tea and folded a basket of laundry, sat down with the newspaper and a book and fell asleep. When didn't he feel tired.

Weeknights, the girls woke him twice, three times, needing something, and P. needed her sleep (Friday night, and Saturday night, he took melatonin[60] and slept through it all).

Really he should have raked leaves. He should have put together a grocery list or looked into things to do through the weekend or made some phone calls. Etc.

He woke with the girls and made a cup of tea and changed diapers and made snacks before they walked to the playground, where they'd stay till after six, S. talking to the moms coming in and out. They wore expensive shoes and pushed Peg Perego® strollers and discussed the quality of private schools.

Then S. and the girls dragged their feet home and

---

[60] S. figured a few years of weekend melatonin use couldn't hurt, though Dr. Weil cautioned about using hormone supplements.

Evening

when P. pulled in the driveway and came up the porch stairs
and dropped her bag, S. was forgotten.

S. knew how to make dinner in fifteen minutes, and then they
ate.

Played.

P. supervised baths and pajamas and read board books, though
the girls wouldn't sit still.

Then bed, and P. had work to finish, and S. needed to get out
of the house (to meet Dennis, to buy a bag of Thai Princess
from a California cannabis club—never mind how it crossed
the country. It cost eighty bucks an eighth). P. would be furi-
ous, if she knew.

S. had promised, a long time ago. He had promised. [61]

---

[61] **Cannabis**

In college, when he dealt, S. knew not to smoke while cutting bricks into the
eighth- or quarter-ounce baggies. He knew not to smoke when people came
by to buy, or when people wanted to stay around his place and shoot the shit
and said, You want to light up?

No. He had things to do, and they'd have to go.

He preferred meeting at the library, or the union, or at a bar, and with only
people who knew someone he knew, and, still, he figured he'd end up selling
to a cop, at some point, even if he was careful, careful, careful. So he never
sold in bulk, though it meant more work. Bulk would mean jail, and S. did
not want to go to jail.

Even then, alcohol upset S.'s stomach.

Caffeine (& ZYRTEC®)

P. scattered the pollen that lay thick on the windshield. It covered the back window, too, but would blow off. The front of her skirt felt sticky from spilled applesauce.

She needed to get moving.

Her keys sat on the car roof.

There.

At the first stoplight, P. dug in her bag. She drank an allergy pill with her coffee. S. had washed her mug, but still it smelled of sour milk. She'd get a new one, or she'd ask S. to do it, maybe, over the weekend.

At the next light, she rubbed base on her cheeks. At the next, some lipstick, and she hoped the gas tank would get her to the office and back.

And he took aspirin or Tylenol® only for a blinding headache, and the summer he broke his wrist. He thought they made him slow and dumb.

Ditto antihistamines.

S. ate at the Food Co-Op in the union. Organic produce and fruit. Hummus. Tabouli. Tofu. He refused meat.

S. kept his hair cut. He wore collar shirts and boat shoes. Glasses. He ran every second day and finished a half-marathon his senior year. He made the Dean's list.

He took a subscription to the *New York Times*, using his student discount, and liked sharp, knowledgeable conversation about national and world affairs. He leaned, on the whole, to a Republican interest in smaller government.

He only smoked[1] when he was alone, at night, late, and only the best of the best, which he bought but never sold. It floated him from his sofa, and his

P. would have a donut the first hour at her desk, with a cup of coffee, and another the next hour, with a cup of coffee, and, maybe another half before lunch, with a cup of coffee. The coffee she brewed fresh from single-serving gourmet packs that went in a machine down the hall. Every floor had one. Each cup took sixty seconds.

The firm used a coffee service that hired adults with mental disabilities to look after the machines and the cups and coffee packs and sweeteners and stirrers and messes.

---

shoes, and some nights helped him sleep. It tasted sweet and smelled richer than his product, organic and heady, like a brush fire on a cool day. No paranoia, just curiosity—about class that morning, for example, and the professor's lateness, maybe, and the coffee stain on his shirt. Like that.

Pot, he told himself, does a body good.

Years later, when California agreed that marijuana can reduce pain, increase appetite, and so on, S. said, Well, duh.

[1] S. started at fourteen, after he enrolled at Indian Spring Prep (with help from Aunt Snooker, recently deceased).

He got pot, then mushrooms, then acid[1] from Opal, who attended the alternative public school, where she could wear flowered skirts and smoke in cars.

And from his new friends, to whom he started selling, S. got his first taste of real cash, which was good, and it went fast on exactly what S. couldn't say.

But S. always worried about getting caught, because he didn't want youthful indiscretions trailing him into a future for which he had plans.

And what would his family, down to the last distant cousin, say?

S. hated the labels he collected at school. He was a Dealer (worse yet—Industrious).

Still, he enjoyed staying three steps ahead of the people who bought, as well as anyone who would bust him, and he expanded, at Georgetown, when he found more money to be made from students complaining about their rejection from Harvard or Princeton or Yale.

When S. looked into an honest line of work, he found beltway political action committees willing to take him on, as an intern, for a year or two, after school, if he did well, at a salary in the mid-teens, to start. No ceiling, they said, though every recruiter wore clothes off the rack.

S. also found he could work as an administrative assistant, book buyer, library assistant, guidance counselor, health administrator, social worker, or teacher, though half those jobs required

The allergy medicine called itself non-drowsy, but it made her tired. The coffee helped, though it made her hands tremble.

Any excuse to get up from her desk for two minutes.

---

certification or an M.A. to start. Or he could go into sales, with which he had some experience. No thanks.

I'm not cut out for sales, S. said to P., who believed him. Useless for work in the real world. Maybe academia, she said, because of his brains. For her, law school might be the path—a salary for them, together, and for the family they'd someday raise. He'd have to stop messing around with that stuff, she said.

Okay, S. said, if you think that's best, and set to work on his Ph.D., knowing no job would come of it, but he could be a house-husband, and stay home, and raise the kids. He'd need a nanny, to help.

[1] LSD

For a long time, S. took LSD, and sometimes sold it, along with mushrooms and peyote.

S. took the really pure stuff, because he liked:

Mirrors, and tracing red hexagons in the fabric of his skin.

The colored trails that followed bodies in motion.

Circles of light that flowed and rippled.

Sounds he could feel in his tongue and could see as Daffy Duck, dancing.

The immense distance between him and the window.

Posters that breathed.

Melting into wet, sun-warmed sod.

Trees as incredibly complex and detailed sculptures that could reveal the true nature of the universe.

Epiphanies.

.

He disliked standing alone, outside his apartment, crying, the rain on his hair and body. He leaned against the tree. He held his penis.

I can't, he said to a man passing.

What, the man said.

I can't, S. said. I can't stop peeing, S. said.

It's the rain, John said, when he found S. It's running down your dick, and he led S. back inside, to the living room, where they looped a video of Pink Floyd at Pompeii.

You're fucked up, John said, and laughed, and S. agreed.

I feel squishy, S. said.

P. spent her days digging through white file-folder boxes filled with originary materials she'd use while drafting one patent license after another after another.

And she received emails from partners and clients, and she spent her days responding.

The real fun, she said to S., came with infringements, where she negotiated differences between widgets from Edison A-hole and Edison B-hole.

When she became partner, she'd litigate the infringement battles in court, which would be better, and she'd schmooze clients at business lunches. She'd hold their hands through the fight and bill every minute.

She'd finally tell partner A to get out of his chair and speak in person with associate B, instead of through email, which they copied her every time.

P. cleaned her desktop, moving Redwelds® to the work tables running along her office walls. She straightened her pens, and her Palm® cradle, and her BlackBerry®, and her dictaphone. She stacked her Post-Its by color.

She thought about a Caesar salad with grilled tuna[62] for lunch, and about the summer associate already famous for her thongs, and the kid from Yale who didn't shake after peeing. Dave the drip.

---

[62] She'd never lose the weight from the girls, and she didn't care, though she didn't want to gain more.

P. called Susan, who—as counsel—made only $100,000 a year, and would always be on contract, because she didn't make partner (but had evenings and weekends free, for her kids).

Not like P.

When P. made non-equity partner, she would earn a quarter of a million a year. When she took ownership of part of the firm, a half million. She'd be one of twelve women partners with children. She'd be tethered to her BlackBerry.

She'd need to bill a minimum of 1,950 hours a year, plus the 50 pro bono, for the rest of her life. That meant 167 a month (plus the pro bono). That meant, really, 50 a week, because that's what it takes.

If that's what it takes, P. said to Susan, who asked her, What?

Sorry, P. said.

P. ordered lunch in, so she wouldn't go off the clock.

P.'s billing sheet split her day into six-minute increments.[63]

63

Sometimes at night, P. clocked the girls' baths, though she didn't mean to.

She drank French roast, with cream. A Splenda®.

When P. got tired, she sweated under her arms. Between her legs.

After lunch, she stayed out of the halls, and conversation.

She answered emails and sent her morning's work to the typing pool and planned her agenda.

She stayed calm about the late-afternoon contracts and started what could be done before evening and set the rest on the floor, to take home.

Acid rose in her throat when she burped, and she breathed the ripeness of lunch and coffee and mints. The lining of her nose hurt. For a second, she felt dizzy. She decided they'd buy the treadmill, for the basement.

P.'s college roommate taught fourth grade and lived in a tiny home in Pittsburgh.

P.'s brother floated from job to job on the West Coast, mostly in hospitality. Wineries.

P.'s girls lived in one of the nation's most cosmopolitan cities. They would attend private schools their entire lives. They'd wear nice clothes.

There would be a beach house.

When P.'s father retired, they'd be able to help him, financially, and maybe buy him a condo.

And S. would plan fun things to do: bluegrass festivals, skiing, weekends in New York. S. always had a plan.

P. loved S. And the girls. She'd see them in a couple of hours, for a couple of hours.

Associates never left before six. It wasn't done. The secretaries left before six.

P. liked doing what needed to be done. It's easy if you set your mind to it.

Ritalin®[1]

Concerta®

The characteristics of ADHD are inattention, hyperactivity, and impulsivity. These symptoms appear early in some children may have these symptoms, but at a low level or the symptoms may be caused by another disorder. It is important that the child receive a thorough examination and appropriate diagnosis by a well qualified professional.

Symptoms of ADHD will appear over the course of many months, often with the symptoms of impulsiveness and hyperactivity preceding those of inattention, which may not emerge for a year or more. Different symptoms may appear in different settings, depending on the demands for the child's self-control. A child who "can't sit still" or is otherwise disruptive will be noticeable in school, but the inattentive daydreamer may be overlooked. The impulsive child who acts before thinking may be seen as just a "discipline problem," while the child who is passive or sluggish may be viewed as merely unmotivated. Yet both may have different types of *(speaker phone)* is with other children, or behavior at home. ADHD may be suspected but because the symptoms...

According to the most recent version of the Diagnostic and Statistical Manual of Mental Disorders (DSM-IV-TR), there are three patterns of behavior that indicate ADHD. People with ADHD may show several signs of being inattentive. They may have a pattern of being hyperactive and impulsive far more than others of their age. Or they may show all three types of behavior. This means that there are three subtypes of ADHD recognized by professionals.

Hyperactive children always seem to be "on the go" or constantly in motion. They dash around touching or playing with whatever is in sight, or talk incessantly. Sitting still at dinner or during a school lesson or story can be a difficult task. They squirm and fidget in their seats or roam around the room. Or they may wriggle their feet, touch everything, or noisily tap their pencil. Hyperactive teenagers or adults may feel internally restless. They often report...

R.[2] Three- or four years. From then. He was active.

U.[5] It's a low dose.

A.[4] Concerta. Eighteen milligrams.

N.[3] Woke up early.

A. We're getting an increase.

U. Yeah.

U. I don't know about that.

[1] Street Terms for Ritalin are:

* Kibbles and bits
* Kiddy cocaine
* Pineapple
* Skippy
* Smarties
* Vitamin R
* West Coast

[2] Responsible party

[3] Next of Kin

[4] Authorizee / Authorized

[5] Undersigned

The principal characteristics of ADHD are inattention, hyperactivity, and impulsivity. These symptoms appear early. **A. Once in the morning. Time release.** at a low level, or the symptoms may be caused by another disorder, it is important that the child receive a thorough examination and appropriate diagnosis by a well-qualified professional.

Symptoms of ADHD will appear over the course of many months, often with the symptoms of impulsiveness and hyperactivity preceding those of inattention, which may not emerge for a year or more. Different symptoms may appear in different settings, depending on the demands the situation may pose for the child's self-control. A child who "can't sit still" or is otherwise disruptive will be noticeable in school, but the inattentive daydreamer may be overlooked. **R. He went to bed, you know, the normal time.** the problem, "while the impulsive child who acts before thinking may be viewed as merely a discipline problem. **U. Yeah.** or sluggish may be misperceived as not motivated. Yet both may have different types of school, social relationships with kind of children, or those for whom. ADHD may be suspected. But because the symptoms vary so much across settings, ADHD is not easy to diagnose. This is especially true when inattentiveness is the primary symptom.

According to the most recent version of the Diagnostic and Statistical Manual of Mental Disorders [DSM-IV-TR] there are three patterns of behavior that indicate ADHD. People with ADHD may show several signs of being **N. One morning we hear him, only he's not in his room.** or of acting on impulse. Or they may show all three types of behavior. The issue that there are subtypes of ADHD recognized by **U. It's an amphetamine.** how significant hyperactive-impulsive behavior/sometimes called impulsivity for a long time that displays both inattentive and hyperactive-impulsive symptoms.

He's saying, Mommy, come look.
Hyperactive children always seem to be "on the go" or constantly in motion. They dash around touching or playing with whatever is in sight, or talk incessantly. Sitting still at dinner or during a school lesson or story can be a difficult task. They squirm and fidget in their seats or roam around the room. Or they may wiggle their feet, touch everything, or noisily tap their pencil. Hyperactive teenagers or adults may feel internally restless. They often report **A. Her schoolwork's changed.** needing to stay busy and may try to do several things at once.

Impulsive children seem unable to curb their immediate reactions or think before they act. They will often blurt out inappropriate comments, display their emotions without restraint, and act without regard for the later consequences of their conduct. Their impulsivity may make it hard for them to wait for things they want or to take their turn in games. They may grab a toy from another child or hit when they're upset. Even as teenagers or adults, they may take **R. He was in the kitchen.** mediate but small payoffs rather than engage in activities that may take more effort yet provide much greater but delayed rewards.

Some signs of hyperactivity-impulsivity are:
* Feeling restless, often fidgeting with hands or feet, or squirming while seated **A. She couldn't sit still. She couldn't watch TV. She couldn't**
* Running, climbing, or leaving a seat in situations where sitting or quiet behavior is expected **read.**
* Blurting out answers before hearing the whole question **N. He was on top of the fridge. He climbed up.**
* Having difficulty waiting in line or taking turns

Children who are inattentive have a hard time keeping their minds on any one thing and may get bored with a task after only a few minutes. If they are doing something they really enjoy, they have no trouble paying attention. But focusing deliberate, conscious attention to organizing and completing a task or learning something new is difficult. **U. She'd sit here, like this. (waves arms and legs)** enthused, is full of ...

Homework is often extraordinarily hard for these children. They will forget to write down an assignment, or leave it at school, or bring it home but forget to do it. They'll forget to bring a book, or bring the wrong one, and lose. **R. He was pretty proud.**

The DSM-IV-TR gives these signs of inattention:

Children diagnosed with the Predominantly Inattentive Type of ADHD are seldom impulsive or hyperactive, yet they have significant problems paying attention. They appear to be daydreaming, "spaced-out," easily confused, slow **R. We put a lock on his door.** Careless mistakes
* Easily distracted by sights and sounds
* Often skipping from one uncompleted task to another **A. Like you.**

Children who are lethargic. They may have difficulty processing information as quickly and accurately as other children. They have trouble in written instructions, a hard time understanding what he or she is **R. On the outside.** nt mistakes. Yet the child may sit quietly, unobtrusively, and even appear to be working, understanding the task and the instructions.

These children don't show significant problems with impulsivity and overactivity in the classroom, on the school ground, or at home. They may get along better with other children than the more impulsive and hyperactive types of ADHD, and they may not have the same sorts of social problems so common with the combined type of ADHD. So often their problems with inattention are overlooked. But they need help just as much as children with other types of ADHD, who cause more obvious problems in the classroom.

R. A chain.

A. We tried Sylvan®.

N. High up. For us.

U. Five grand.

R. For his safety. The doctor said.

U. We paid them guys five grand.

N. He could call from his room: Play until we got up.

U. Up front. We wrote a check.

A. Could of lit a fire under that money.

N. At school.

A. People don't want to put their kids on meds.

R. The teachers called him from the room.

A. We looked online for diets.

A. We bought drops. What were they. Focus®. We gave them to her mornings and evenings.

R. He had a terrible temper.

N. He got frustrated. <small>...are inattention, hyperactivity, and impulsivity. These symptoms appear early in... may be caused by another disorder. It is important that the child receive a thorough combination and appropriate diagnosis by a well qualified professional.</small>

U. We tried fish oil. <small>...when they have these symptoms, but at a low level, or the symptoms may appear in different settings, depending on the demands the situation may pose for the child's self-control. A child who "can't sit still" or is otherwise disruptive will be noticeable in school, but the inattentive daydreamer may be... Yet both may have different types of... school, social relationships with other children, or behavior at home, ADHD may be suspected. But because the symptoms vary so much across settings, ADHD is not easy to diagnose. This is especially true when inattentiveness is the primary symptom.</small>

R. Threw things. <small>Symptoms of ADHD will appear over the course of many months, often with the symptoms of impulsiveness and hyperactivity preceding those of inattention, which may not emerge for a year or more. Different symptoms may appear in different settings, depending on the demands the situation may pose for the child's self control. A child who "can't sit still" or is otherwise disruptive will be noticeable in school, but the inattentive daydreamer may be... sometimes act without thinking, sometimes daydream the time away. When the child's... distractibility, poor concentration, or impulsivity begin to affect performance in school, social relationships with other children, or behavior at home. ADHD may be suspected. But because the symptoms vary so much across settings. ADHD is not easy to diagnose. This is especially true when inattentiveness is the primary symptom.</small>

A. Fish oil.

U. The doctor told us to try coffee (*laughs*). Her teacher threw a fit. Said don't ever try that on me. <small>According to the most recent version of the Diagnostic and Statistical Manual of Mental Disorders (DSM-IV-TR), there are three patterns of behavior that indicate ADHD. People with ADHD may show several signs of being consistently inattentive. They may have a pattern of being hyperactive and impulsive far more than others of their age. Or they may show all three types of behavior... These are the predominantly hyperactive-impulsive type (that does not show significant inattention); the predominantly inattentive type (that does not show significant hyperactive-impulsive behavior, sometimes called ADD—an outdated term for this entire disorder); and the combined type (that displays both inattentive and hyperactive-impulsive symptoms).</small>

R. He couldn't sit still. <small>Hyperactive children always seem to be "on the go" or constantly in motion. They dash around touching or playing with whatever is in sight, or talk incessantly. Sitting still through dinner or during a school lesson or story can be a difficult task. They squirm and fidget in their seats or roam around the room. Or they may wiggle their feet, touch everything, or noisily tap their pencil. Hyperactive teenagers or adults may feel internally restless. They often report needing to stay busy and may try to do several things at once.</small>

A. (*laughs*) Mrs. Klaus. She said stop experimenting on me. <small>Impulsive children seem unable to curb their immediate reactions or think before they act. They will often blurt out inappropriate comments, display their emotions without restraint, and act without regard for the later consequences of their conduct. Their impulsivity may make it hard for them to wait for things they want or to take their turn in games. They may grab a toy from another child or hit when they are upset. Even as teenagers or adults, they may impulsively choose to do things that have an immediate but small payoff rather than engage in activities that may take more effort but that provide greater but delayed rewards.</small>

R. Even finish a meal. <small>
- Feeling restless, often fidgeting with hands or feet, or squirming while seated
- Running, climbing, or leaving a seat in situations where sitting or quiet behavior is expected
- Blurting out answers before hearing the whole question
- Having difficulty waiting in line or taking turns.</small>

<small>Children who are inattentive have a hard time keeping their minds on any one thing and may get bored with a task after only a few minutes. They may give effortless, automatic attention to organizing and completing a task or learning something new is difficult.</small>

A. She said don't pack her a backpack. <small>...no trouble paying attention. For...</small>

<small>Homework is particularly hard for these children. They will forget to write down an assignment, or leave it at school. They will forget to bring a book home, or bring the wrong one. The homework, if finally finished, is full of errors and erasures. Homework is often accompanied by frustration for both parent and child.</small>

N. He drove his brother nuts. <small>
- Often becoming easily distracted by irrelevant sights and sounds
- Often failing to pay attention to details and making careless mistakes
- Rarely following instructions carefully and completely losing or forgetting things like toys, or pencils, books, and tools needed for a task.</small>

U. (*sits up*) Yeah. Cause she digs into it all the time.

R. His brother, you could sit him down with a pen and paper. <small>These children don't show signs and problems with impulsivity and overactivity in the classroom, on the school grounds... Some children only have the inattentive type of ADHD... these children are not overly active. They do not disrupt the classroom or other activities, so their symptoms may not be noticed. Among children with ADHD, the inattentive type is more common in girls than in boys. The inattentive child... has difficulty processing information as quickly and accurately as other children. When the teacher gives oral or even written instructions, this child has a hard time understanding what he or she is supposed to be working on but not fully attending to or understanding the task and the instructions.</small>

A. Focused on anything but the teacher. <small>These children don't show enough signs and problems with impulsivity and overactivity... the same sorts of social problems so common with the combined type of ADHD. So they may be overlooked, and even their parents may not notice that... impulsive, so many... easily confused, slow moving... and they may not have the same sorts of social problems so common with the combined type of ADHD. So they may... the different types of ADHD, and that they may not be as much as children with other types of ADHD, who cause more obvious problems in the classroom.</small>

U. But I don't want to up her dose.

The principal characteristics of ADHD are inattention, hyperactivity, and impulsivity. These symptoms appear early... These symptoms appear early, but at a low level, or the symptoms may be caused by another disorder. It is important that the child receive a thorough examination and appropriate diagnosis by a well-qualified professional.

A. The first week was scary.

Symptoms of ADHD will appear over the course of many months, often with the symptoms of impulsiveness and hyperactivity preceding those of inattention, which may not emerge for a year or more. Different symptoms may appear in different settings, depending on the demands the situation may pose for the child's self-control. A child who "can't sit still" or is otherwise disruptive will be noticeable in school, but be inconspicuous or overlooked in... A child who acts before thinking may be considered just a "discipline problem," while the child who is passive or sluggish may be viewed as merely unmotivated. Yet both may have different types of ADHD. All children are sometimes restless, sometimes act without thinking, sometimes daydream the time away. When the child's hyperactivity, distractibility, poor concentration, or impulsivity begin to affect performance in school, social relationships with other children, or behavior at home, ADHD may be suspected. But because the symptoms vary so much across settings, ADHD is not easy to diagnose. This is especially true when inattentiveness is the primary symptom.

N. Was it hard.

U. Yeah. She looked like someone on something.

According to the most recent version of the Diagnostic and Statistical Manual of Mental Disorders 2 (DSM-IV-TR), there are three primary subtypes of behavior that indicate ADHD. People with ADHD may show several signs of being... They may have a pattern of being hyperactive and impulsive far more than others of their age. Or they may show... the three subtypes of ADHD recognized by the... called ADHD—predominantly hyperactive-impulsive type (that does not show significant inattention), the predominantly inattentive type (that displays both inattentive and hyperactive-impulsive behaviors) sometimes...
- Hyperactivity-Impulsivity

R. Was it hard.

A. She wouldn't eat. She couldn't sleep.

Hyperactive children always seem to be "on the go" or constantly in motion. They dash around touching or playing with whatever is in sight, or talk incessantly. Sitting still at dinner or during a school lesson or story can be a... difficult task. They squirm and fidget in their seats or roam around the room. Or they may wiggle their feet, touch everything, or noisily tap their pencil. They also may feel intensely restless. They often report out...

R. A lot of anger.

U. She was speeded out.

Impulsive children seem unable to curb their immediate reactions or think before they act. They will often blurt out inappropriate comments, display their emotions without restraint, and act without regard for the later consequences of their conduct. Their impulsivity may make it hard for them to wait for things they want or to take their turn in games. They may grab a toy from another child or hit when they're upset. Even as teenagers or adults, they may impulsively choose to do things that have an immediate, but small payoff rather than engage in activities that may take more effort yet provide much greater but delayed rewards.

R. Unpleasant.

Impulsivity can be:
- Feeling restless, often fidgeting with hands or feet, or squirming while seated
- Running, climbing, or leaving a seat in situations where sitting or quiet behavior is expected
- Blurting out answers before hearing the whole question
- Having difficulty waiting in line or taking turns

A. She sat and crocheted.

N. I'm not the most patient man.

It can be tiny one thing and may get bored with a task after only a few minutes. If they are doing something they really enjoy, they have no trouble paying attention. But focusing deliberate, conscious attention to organizing and completing a task or learning something new is difficult.

Homework is particularly hard for these children. They will forget to write down an assignment, or leave it at school. They will forget to bring a book home, or bring the wrong one. The homework, if finally finished, is full of errors and erasures. Homework is often accompanied by frustration for both parent and child.

R. It took a lot of energy.

A. She does those long tails.

Children diagnosed with the Predominantly Inattentive Type of ADHD are seldom impulsive or hyperactive, yet they have significant problems paying attention. They appear to be daydreaming, "spacey," easily confused, slow moving, and lethargic. They may have difficulty processing information as quickly and accurately as other children. When the teacher gives oral or even written instructions, the child has a hard time understanding what he or she is supposed to do and makes frequent mistakes. Yet the child may sit quietly, unobtrusively, and even appear to be working but not fully attending to or understanding the task and the instructions.

U. She made one longer than the sofa *(both laugh)*.

These children don't show significant problems with impulsivity and overactivity in the classroom, on the school grounds, or at home. They may not get along as well with other children as the more impulsive and hyperactive types of ADHD, and they may not have the same sorts of social problems so common with the combined type of ADHD. So often... When the teacher appears to be daydreaming... types and types of ADHD, who cause more obvious problems in the classroom.

A. But now she's like normal. She eats. She grazes.

R. I did the Feingold® diet. Cleaned out the house. All the *early* U. I was gonna yank her off. *those symptoms, but at a lower level, or the symptoms*

may be caused by another disorder, it is important that the child receive a thorough examination and appropriate diagnosis by a well-qualified professional.

sugary foods, the artificial coloring. *often with the symptoms of impulsiveness and hyperactivity pervading these areas of inattention, which may not emerge for a year or more. Different symptoms may appear in different settings, depending on the demands the child may pose for the child's self-control. A child who "can't sit still" or is otherwise disruptive will be noticeable in a minute daycare or may be overlooked. The impulsive child who acts before thinking may be considered a "discipline problem," while the child who is passive or daydreams may be overlooked. ADHD. All children are sometimes restless, sometimes act without thinking, sometimes daydream the time away. When ADHD may be suspected. But because the symptoms vary so much across settings, ADHD is not easy to diagnose. This is typically the job when inattentiveness is school, too.*

N. It helped. now.

The most recent version of the Diagnostic and Statistical Manual of Mental Disorders (DSM-IV-TR), there A. But she's focused. She's like herself, only she's reading *are three patterns of behavior that indicate ADHD. People with ADHD may show several signs of being consistently inattentive. They may have a pattern of being hyperactive and impulsive far more than others of their age. Or they may show all three types of behavior. This means that there are three subtypes of ADHD recognized by professionals. These are the predominantly hyperactive-impulsive type (that does not show significant inattention), the predominantly inattentive type (that does not show significant hyperactivity-impulsivity or behavior) sometimes called ADD—an outdated term for this entire disorder, and the combined type (that displays both inattentive and hyperactive-impulsive symptoms.)*

R. It helped, but when he got to third grade, he was barely U. We were big readers. Before all this (*waves at the room*).

Hyperactive children always seem to be "on the go" or constantly in motion. They dash around touching or playing with whatever is in sight, or talk incessantly. Sitting still at dinner or room in class can be a task they find impossible. They squirm and fidget in their seats or roam around the room. Or they may wiggle their feet, touch everything, or noisily tap their pencil. Hyperactive teenagers or adults may feel internally restless. They often report reading. *needing to stay busy and may try to do several things at once.*

U. I didn't want her on medicine. It's copping out, putting

Impulsive children seem unable to curb their immediate reactions or think before they act. They will often blurt out inappropriate comments, or display their emotions without restraint, and act without regard for the later consequences of their conduct. Their impulsivity may make it hard for them to wait for things they want or to take their turn in games. They may grab a toy from another child or hit when they're upset. Even as teenagers or adults, they may kids on drugs. *impulsively choose to do things that have an immediate but small payoff rather than engage in activities that may take more effort but provide greater but delayed rewards.*

N. We called our friend. A doctor at UCLA.

* Feeling restless, often fidgeting with hands or feet, or squirming while seated
* Running, climbing, or leaving a seat, in situations where sitting or quiet behavior is expected A. Her cousin's on Strattera®. *enjoy, they have no trouble paying attention. But*
* Blurting out answers before hearing the whole question
* Having difficulty awaiting in line or taking turns.

R. Psychologist. *have a hard time keeping their minds on any one thing and may get bored with a task after* *just a few minutes, enjoy, they have no trouble paying attention. But* *focusing deliberate, conscious attention to organizing and completing a task or learning something new is difficult.*

Homework is particularly hard for these children. They will forget to write down an assignment, or leave it at school. They will forget to bring a book home, or bring the wrong one. The homework, if finally finished, is full of N. And he put us in touch with the head guy at Children's *errors and erasures. Homework is often accompanied by frustration for both parent and child.*

Psychology. *easily distracted by irrelevant sights and sounds*
* Rarely following instructions carefully and completely losing or forgetting things like toys, or pencils, books, and tools needed for a task A. She's gonna be on it till end of high school. Or junior
* Rarely giving attention to details and making careless mistakes
* Often skipping from one uncompleted activity to another.

Children diagnosed with the Predominantly Inattentive Type of ADHD are seldom impulsive or hyperactive, yet they have significant problems paying attention. They appear to be daydreaming, "spacey," easily confused, slow R. Psychiatry. *moving, and lethargic. They may have difficulty processing information as quickly and accurately as other children. When the teacher gives oral or even written instructions, this child has a hard time understanding what he or she is* high. *supposed to do, and makes frequent mistakes. Yet the child may sit quietly, unobtrusively, and even appear to be working, fully attending to or understanding the task and the instructions.*

These children don't show significant problems with impulsivity and overactivity in the classroom, on the school ground, or at home. They may get along better with other children than the more impulsive ones who have ADHD, and they may not have the same sorts of social problems so common with the combined type of ADHD. So often their problems with inattention are overlooked. But they need help just as much as children with other types of ADHD, who cause more obvious problems in the classroom.

R. He asked questions. What happens, when. What happens if.

* ADHD will appear over the course of many months, often with the symptoms of impulsiveness and hyperactivity preceding those of inattention, which may not emerge for a year or more. Different symptoms may appear in different settings, depending on the demands the situation may pose for the child's self-control. A child who "can't sit still" or is otherwise disruptive will be noticeable in school, but be unnoticeable at home.

ADHD. All children are sometimes restless, sometimes act without thinking, sometimes daydream the time away. When ... ADHD may be suspected. But because the symptoms vary so much to try settings, ADHD is not easy to diagnose. This is especially true when ...

school, social relationships with other children, or behavior at home, ADHD may be suspected.

N. And we said he could concentrate. When he wanted.

According to the most recent version of the Diagnostic and Statistical Manual of Mental Disorders (DSM-IV-TR), there are three patterns of behavior that indicate ADHD. People with ADHD may show several signs of being consistently inattentive. They may have a pattern of being hyperactive and impulsive far more than others of their age. Or they may show three subtypes of ADHD recognized by professional. These are the predominantly hyperactive-impulsive type (that does not show significant inattention), the predominantly inattentive type (that does not show significant hyperactivity-impulsivity) and the combined type (that displays both inattentive and hyperactive-impulsive symptoms).

R. He couldn't sit still. He was overactive.

Hyperactive children almost always seem to be in motion. ... They dash around touching or playing with whatever is in sight, or talk incessantly. Sitting still at dinner or during a school lesson or story can be a difficult task. They squirm and fidget in their seats or roam around the room. Or they may wiggle their feet, touch everything, or noisily tap their pencil. Hyperactive teenagers or adults may feel internally restless. They often report needing to stay busy and may try to do several things at once.

N. Hyperactive.

Impulsive children seem unable to curb their immediate reactions or think before they act. They will often blurt out inappropriate comments, display their emotions without restraint, and act without regard for the later consequences of their conduct. Their impulsivity may make it hard for them to wait for things they want or to take their turn in games. They may grab a toy from another child or hit when they're upset. Even as teenagers or adults, they may ... things ... now effort yet provide much greater but delayed rewards.

Some signs of hyperactivity-impulsivity are:

* Feeling restless, often fidgeting with hands or feet, or squirming while seated
* Running, climbing, or leaving a seat in situations where sitting or quiet behavior is expected
* Blurting out answers before hearing the whole question
* Having difficulty waiting in line or taking turns.

R. They prescribed Ritalin.

Children who are inattentive have a hard time keeping their minds on any one thing and may get bored with a task after only a few minutes ... if they ... are ... doing something ... they enjoy ... Giving focused attention to organizing and completing a task or learning something new is difficult.

Homework is particularly hard for these children. They will forget to write down an assignment, or leave it at school. Or ... get to bring a book home, or bring the wrong one. The homework, if finally finished, is full of errors and erasures. Homework is often accompanied by frustration for both parent and child.

The DSM-IV-TR gives these signs of inattention:

N. It's a stimulant.

* Becoming easily distracted by irrelevant sights and sounds
* Failing to pay attention to details and making careless mistakes
* Rarely following instructions carefully and completely losing or forgetting things like toys, or pencils, books, and tools needed for a task
* Often skipping from one uncompleted activity to another.

Children diagnosed with the Predominantly Inattentive Type of ADHD are seldom impulsive or hyperactive, yet they have significant problems paying attention. They appear to be daydreaming, "spacey," easily confused, slow moving, and lethargic. They may have difficulty processing information as quickly and accurately as other children. ... the child has a hard time understanding what he or she is supposed to do and makes frequent mistakes. Yet the child may sit quietly, unobtrusively, and even appear to be working, but not be fully attending to the task and the instructions.

These children don't show significant problems with impulsivity and overactivity in the classroom, on the school ground, or at home. They may get along better with other children than the more impulsive and hyperactive types of ADHD, and they may not have the same sorts of social problems so common with the combined type of ADHD. So often their problems with inattention are overlooked. But they need help just as much as children with other types of ADHD, who cause more obvious problems in the classroom.

A. The teacher fills out paperwork the doctor gives you.

A. It's multiple choice. Like a survey.

A. We took her to a counselor in second grade.

A. (points at U.) The doctor said I know where she gets it from.

U. (laughs) He took one look at me.

A. He tried Strattera.

R. For kids with ADD, it has a reverse effect on the... U. (serious) Yeah. I had a bad reaction.

blood.

U. They gave me drugs to go the other way.

R. It calms them down.

U. (sprawls on sofa) Man, I looked stoned. (laughs) Like I smoked a big stack.

R. We waited until the weekend.

N. His brother and I went camping.

A. When we were in Riverside.

R. You went to the Indian Guides in Sacramento.[4]

U. I didn't want to put her on it. Speed, right. I thought she's so tiny. She'd shrink.

A. We didn't want to change her personality.

N. We were gone.

U. We didn't want her to walk around like a zombie.

R. I gave him the pill, and he took it, and we waited, and then we sat down and played a game.

U. She's my boo boo.

R: We played the whole game.

U: So we gave Sylvan five grand.

N: I called, and R. said, I gave him the pill, and we're sitting here playing a game.

U: They had a money-back guarantee. It said so on the commercials. If you don't see an improvement.

R: He didn't get distracted. Or angry. Because he would get angry.

U: Then we looked at the fine print. Didn't apply in our region.

N: They were actually sitting there, playing a game.

U: Five thousand bucks.

N: It has a place. The drug.

R: I thought I would cry.

A: His oldest daughter. She was on Adderall®.

N: It was a big deal.

U: Yeah. She lost twenty-five pounds.

N: She said, We just played a whole game.

U: She was up at midnight cleaning the baseboards. With a toothbrush.

The principal characteristics of ADHD are inattention, hyperactivity, and impulsivity. These symptoms appear early in a child's life. Since many normal children may have these symptoms, but at a low level, or the symptoms may be caused by another disorder, it is important that the child receive a thorough examination and appropriate diagnosis by a well-qualified professional.

U. She could lose it, though.

Symptoms of ADHD will appear over the course of many months, often with the symptoms of impulsiveness and hyperactivity preceding those of inattention, which may not emerge for a year or more. Different symptoms may appear in different settings, depending on the demands the situation may pose for the child's self-control. A child who "can't sit still" or is otherwise disruptive will be noticeable in school, but the inattentive daydreamer may be overlooked. The impulsive child who acts before thinking may be considered just a "discipline problem," while the child who is passive or sluggish may be viewed as merely unmotivated. Yet both may have different types of ADHD. All children are sometimes restless, sometimes act without thinking, sometimes daydream the time away. But the child with ADHD... poor concentration and impulsivity... ADHD may be suspected... at home. ADHD may be suspected. But because the symptoms vary so much across settings, ADHD is not easy to diagnose. This is especially true when inattentiveness is the primary symptom.

R. That was a big moment.

U. The weight.

According to the most recent version of the Diagnostic and Statistical Manual of Mental Disorders? (DSM-IV-TR) there are three patterns of behavior that indicate ADHD. People with ADHD may show several signs of being inattentive. And they may have a pattern of being hyperactive and impulsive far more than others of their age. Or they may show all three types of behavior. This means that there are three subtypes of ADHD recognized by professionals. These are the predominantly hyperactive-impulsive type (that does not show significant inattention); the predominantly inattentive type (that does not show significant hyperactive-impulsive behavior) sometimes called ADD; and the combined type (that displays both inattentive and hyperactive-impulsive symptoms).

Hyperactivity-Impulsivity

N. That was big.

A. She's a big girl.

Hyperactive children always seem to be "on the go" or constantly in motion. They dash around touching or playing with whatever is in sight, or talk incessantly. Sitting still at dinner or during a school lesson or story can be a difficult task. They squirm and fidget in their seats or roam around the room. Or they may wiggle their feet, touch everything, or noisily tap their pencil.

Impulsive children seem unable to curb their immediate reactions or think before they act. They will often blurt out inappropriate comments, display their emotions without restraint, and act without regard for the later consequences of their conduct. Their impulsivity may make it hard for them to wait for things they want or to take their turn in games. They may grab a toy from another child or hit when they're upset. Even as teenagers or adults, they may impulsively choose to do things that have an immediate but small payoff.

U. (laughs) Yeah. She'd thump the boys. (laughs) She'd find the bullies and thump 'em.

R. Don't think I wasn't scared. This was a new thing then.

* Feel restless, often fidgeting with hands or feet, or squirming while seated
* Running, climbing, or leaving a seat in situations where sitting or quiet behavior is expected
* Blurt out answers before hearing the whole question
* Have difficulty waiting in line or taking turns.

They hadn't used it a lot.

A. They didn't see her coming.

Children who are inattentive have a hard time keeping their minds on any one thing and may get bored with a task after only a few minutes. If they are doing something they really enjoy, they have no trouble paying attention. But focusing deliberate, conscious attention to organizing and completing a task or learning something new is difficult. *(both laugh)*

R. It affects your liver.

* Often get easily distracted by irrelevant sights and sounds
* Often fail to pay attention to details and make careless mistakes
* Rarely follow instructions carefully and completely; losing or forgetting things like toys, or pencils, books, and tools needed for a task
* Often skipping from one uncompleted activity to another.

The DSM-IV-TR gives these signs of inattention.

R. It made his stomach hurt. He had no appetite.

Children diagnosed with the Predominantly Inattentive Type of ADHD are seldom impulsive or hyperactive, yet they have significant problems paying attention. They appear to be daydreaming, "spacey," easily confused, slow moving, and sluggish. They may have difficulty processing information as quickly and accurately as other children. When the teacher gives oral or written instructions, this child has a hard time or even instructions this child has a hard time understanding what he or she is to do and makes numerous errors.

N. Which he was already skin and bones.

These children don't show significant problems with impulsivity and overactivity in the classroom, on the school ground, or at home. They may get along better with other children than the more impulsive and hyperactive types of ADHD, and they may not have the same sorts of social problems so common with the combined type of ADHD. So often their problems with inattention are overlooked. But they just don't get help. Instead, they are children with other types of ADHD, who cause more obvious problems in the classroom.

A. Yeah. She was living with us then.

R: But it worked.

U: She was on Ritalin® when she lived with her mom.

N: It worked.

A: Then she came to live with us.

A: It was, like, 2000.

R: He did better in school.

U: Yeah. We saw how it affected her.

R: Better focus.

U: But I wish we'd done it sooner. This time.

U: This works better.*

A: It works.

R: He had to take it every four hours.

N: He didn't like that.

U: Yeah.

N: At school.

* Brand names of drugs that contain methylphenidate include Ritalin (Ritalina®, Rilatine®, Ritaline®, Ritalin LA® (Long Acting)), Attenta®, Concerta (a timed-release capsule), Metadate®, Methylin® and Rubifen®.

R. He had to go to the nurse to get it. Which made him feel.

maybe caused by another disorder, it is important that the child receive a thorough examination and appropriate diagnosis by a well-qualified professional

Symptoms of ADHD will appear over the course of many months, often with the symptoms of impulsiveness and hyper-activity preceding those of inattention, which may not appear for a year or more. Different symptoms may appear in different settings, depending on the demands the situation may pose for the child's self-control. A child who "can't sit still" or is otherwise disruptive will be noticeable in school, but the inattentive daydreamer may be overlooked. The impulsive child who acts before thinking may be considered just a "discipline problem," while the child who is passive or sluggish may be viewed as merely unmotivated. Yet both may have different types of ADHD. All children are sometimes restless, sometimes act without thinking, sometimes daydream the time away. When the child's hyperactivity, distractibility, poor concentration, or impulsivity begin to affect performance in school, social relationships with other children, or behavior at home, ADHD may be suspected. But because the symptoms vary so much across settings, ADHD is not easy to diagnose. This is especially true when inattentiveness is

N. You know.

U. (*points at the TV.*) Can you believe them guys drive around looking for twisters.

According to the most recent version of the Diagnostic and Statistical Manual of Mental Disorders 2 (DSM-IV-TR), there are three patterns of behavior that indicate ADHD. People with ADHD may show several signs of being consistently inattentive. They may have a pattern of being hyperactive and impulsive far more than others of their age. Or they may show all three types of behavior. This means that there are three subtypes of ADHD recognized by professionals. These are the predominantly hyperactive-impulsive type (that does not show significant inattention); the predominantly inattentive type (that does not show significant hyperactive-impulsive behavior)—also called ADD—and the combined type (that displays both inattentive and hyperactive-impulsive behavior).

Hyperactivity-Impulsivity

Hyperactive children always seem to be "on the go" or constantly in motion. They dash around touching or playing with whatever is in sight, or talk incessantly. Sitting still at dinner or during a school lesson can be a difficult task. They squirm and fidget in their seats or roam around the room. Or they may wriggle their feet, touch everything, noisily tap their pencil. Hyperactive teenagers or adults may feel internally restless. They often report needing to stay busy and may try to do several things at once.

N. It worked.

U. The Weather Channel®.

Some signs of hyperactivity-impulsivity are:

* Feeling restless, often fidgeting with hands or feet, or squirming while seated
* Running, climbing, or leaving a seat in situations where sitting or quiet behavior is expected

N. Grades. Everything. At home.

Children who are inattentive have a hard time keeping their minds on any one thing and may get bored with a task after only a few minutes. Focusing conscious, deliberate attention to organizing and completing a task or learning something new is difficult.

R. It worked.

U. This and Discovery®.

Here are some signs of inattention in children: They will forget to write down an assignment, or leave it at school. They will forget to bring a book home, or bring the wrong one. The homework, if finally finished, is full of errors and erasures. Homework is often accompanied by frustration for both parent and child.

A. The boys love Planet Earth® on Discovery.

The DSM-IV-TR gives these signs of inattention:

* Often becoming easily distracted by irrelevant sights and sounds
* Often failing to pay attention to details and making careless mistakes
* Rarely following instructions carefully and completely losing or forgetting things like toys, or pencils, books, and tools needed for a task
* Often skipping from one uncompleted activity to another

U. You seen it.

Children diagnosed with the Predominantly Inattentive Type of ADHD are seldom impulsive or hyperactive, yet they have significant problems paying attention. They appear to be daydreaming, "spacey," easily confused, slow moving, and lethargic. They may have difficulty processing information as quickly and accurately as other children. When the teacher gives oral or even written instructions, this child has a hard time understanding what he or she is supposed to do and makes frequent mistakes. Yet the child may sit quietly, unobtrusively, and even appear to be working but not fully attending to or understanding the task and the instructions.

These children don't show significant problems with impulsivity and overactivity in the classroom, on the school grounds, or at home. They may get along better with other children than the more impulsive and hyperactive types of ADHD, and they may not have the same sorts of social problems so common with the combined type of ADHD. So often, the problems of children with the inattentive type of ADHD, who cause more obvious problems in the classroom.

U. It's over now, but you can get it on DVD.

The principal characteristics of ADHD are inattention, hyperactivity, and impulsivity. These symptoms appear early in a child's life. Because many normal children may have these symptoms, but at a low level, or the symptoms may be caused by another disorder, it is important that the child receive a thorough examination and appropriate diagnosis by a well-qualified professional.

Symptoms of ADHD will appear over the course of many months, often with the symptoms of impulsiveness and hyperactivity preceding those of inattention. Different symptoms may appear in different settings, depending on the demands the situation may pose for the child's self-control. A child who "can't sit still" or is otherwise disruptive will be noticeable in school, but the inattentive daydreamer may be overlooked. The impulsive child who acts before thinking may be considered just a "discipline problem," while the child who is passive or sluggish may be viewed as merely unmotivated. Yet both may have different types of ADHD. All children are sometimes restless, sometimes act without thinking, sometimes daydream the time away. When the child's hyperactivity, distractibility, poor concentration, or impulsivity begin to affect performance in school, social relationships with other children, or behavior at home, ADHD may be suspected. But because the symptoms vary so much across settings, ADHD is not easy to diagnose. This is especially true when inattentiveness is the primary symptom.

According to the most recent version of the Diagnostic and Statistical Manual of Mental Disorders-2 (DSM-IV-TR) there are three patterns of behavior that indicate ADHD. People with ADHD may show several signs of being consistently inattentive. They may have a pattern of being hyperactive and impulsive far more than others of their age. Or they may show all three types of behavior. ... The means that there are three subtypes of ADHD recognized by professionals. There are the predominantly hyperactive-impulsive type (that does not show significant inattention); the predominantly inattentive type (that does not show significant hyperactive-impulsive behavior) sometimes called ADD — an outdated term for this entire disorder; and the combined type (that displays both inattention and hyperactive-impulsive symptoms.)

Hyperactive children always seem to be "on the go" or constantly in motion. They dash around touching or playing with whatever is in sight, or talk incessantly. ...

Impulsive children seem unable to curb their immediate reactions or think before they act. They will often blurt out inappropriate comments, ...

N. Who wants to be on drugs.

N. If he didn't want to take it, he found a way.

R. He got in some trouble.

R. I don't remember, exactly.

R. Much of 'it I I don't remember, really.

R. We had a busy family.

N. It was a lot.

Symptoms of ADHD will appear over the course of many months, often with the symptoms of impulsiveness and hyperactivity preceding those of inattention, which may not emerge for a year or more. Different symptoms may appear in different settings, depending on the demands the situation may pose for the child's self-control. A child who "can't sit still" or is otherwise disruptive will be noticeable in school, but the inattentive daydreamer may be overlooked. The impulsive child who acts before thinking may be considered just a "discipline problem," while the child who is passive or sluggish may be viewed as merely unmotivated. Yet both may have different types of ADHD. When the child's hyperactivity, distractibility, poor concentration, or impulsivity begin to affect performance in school, social relationships with other children, or behavior at home, ADHD may be suspected. But because the symptoms vary so much across settings, ADHD is not easy to diagnose. This is especially true when inattentiveness is the primary symptom.

R. It was twenty, thirty years ago.

According to the most recent version of the Diagnostic and Statistical Manual of Mental Disorders-2 (DSM-IV-TR), there are three patterns of behavior that indicate ADHD. People with ADHD may show several signs of being consistently inattentive. They may have a pattern of being hyperactive and impulsive far more than others of their age. Or they may show all three types of behavior. The means that there are three subtypes of ADHD recognized by professionals. These are the predominantly hyperactive-impulsive type (that does not show significant inattention), the predominantly inattentive type (that does not show significant hyperactive-impulsive behavior) sometimes called ADD, and the combined type (that displays both inattentive and hyperactive-impulsive symptoms).

• Hyperactivity-Impulsivity

Hyperactive children always seem to be "on the go" or constantly in motion. They dash around touching or playing with whatever is in sight, or talk incessantly. Sitting still at dinner or during a school lesson or story can be a difficult task. They squirm and fidget in their seats or roam around the room. Or they may wiggle their feet, touch everything, or noisily tap their pencil. Hyperactive teenagers or adults may feel intensely restless. They often report a need to stay busy and may try to do several things at once.

Impulsive children seem unable to curb their immediate reactions or think before they act. They will often blurt out inappropriate comments, display their emotions without restraint, and act without regard for the later consequences of their conduct. Their impulsivity may make it hard for them to wait for things they want or to take their turn in games. They may grab a toy from another child or hit when they're upset. Even as teenagers or adults, they may impulsively choose to do things that have an immediate but small payoff rather than engage in activities that may take more effort yet provide much greater but delayed rewards.

R. But he went to college.

Some signs of hyperactivity-impulsivity are:
• Feeling restless, often fidgeting with hands or feet, or squirming while seated
• Running, climbing, or leaving a seat in situations where sitting or quiet behavior is expected
• Blurting out answers before hearing the whole question
• Having difficulty waiting in line or taking turns

R. He finished at Cal Poly. He has a degree from Cal Poly.

• Inattention

Children who are inattentive have a hard time keeping their minds on any one thing and may get bored with a task after only a few minutes. If they are doing something they really enjoy, they have no trouble paying attention. But focusing deliberate, conscious attention to organizing and completing a task or learning something new is difficult.

R. He's a national sales rep for a local TV station in Seattle.

Homework is particularly hard for these children. They will forget to write down an assignment, or leave it at school. They will forget to bring a book home, or bring the wrong one. The homework, if finally finished, is full of errors and erasures. Homework is often accompanied by frustration for both parent and child.

The DSM-IV-TR gives these signs of inattention:

R. He always had the street smarts.

Some signs of inattention are:
• Becoming easily distracted by irrelevant sights and sounds
• Failing to pay attention to details and making careless mistakes
• Rarely following instructions carefully and completely losing or forgetting things like toys, or pencils, books, and tools needed for a task
• Often skipping from one uncompleted activity to another

N. Doesn't take anything now.

Children diagnosed with the Predominantly Inattentive Type of ADHD are seldom impulsive or hyperactive, yet they have significant problems paying attention. They appear to be daydreaming, "spacey," easily confused, slow moving, and apathetic. They may have difficulty processing information as quickly and accurately as other children. When the teacher gives oral or even written instructions, this child has a hard time understanding what he or she is supposed to do and makes frequent mistakes. Yet the child may sit quietly, unobtrusively, and even appear to be working but not fully attending to or understanding the task and the instructions.

These children don't show significant problems with impulsivity and overactivity in the classroom, on the school ground, or at home. They may get along better with other children than do the more impulsive ones with ADHD, and they may not have the same sorts of social problems so common with the combined type of ADHD. So often their problems with inattention are overlooked. But they need help just as much as children with other types of ADHD, who cause more obvious problems in the classroom.

N. Since junior high. ...inattention, hyperactivity, and impulsivity. These symptoms appear early in a child's life. Because many normal children may have these symptoms, but at a lower level, or the symptoms may be caused by another disorder, it is important that the child receive a thorough examination and appropriate diagnosis by a well-qualified professional.

Symptoms of ADHD will appear over the course of many months, often with the symptoms of impulsiveness and hyperactivity preceding those of inattention, which may not emerge for a year or more. Different symptoms may appear in different settings, depending on the demands the situation may pose for the child's self-control. A child who "can't sit still" or is otherwise disruptive will be noticeable in school, but the inattentive daydreamer may be overlooked. The impulsive child who darts across the street or the child who plays dangerously may be more likely to be disciplined. Yet both may have different types of ADHD.

R. He figured out how to manage. ...thinking, sometimes daydream the time away. When the child's hyperactivity, distractibility, poor concentration, or impulsivity begin to affect performance in school, learning disabilities, or behavior problems, ADHD may be suspected. But because the symptoms vary so much across settings, ADHD is not easy to diagnose. This is especially true when inattentiveness is the primary symptom.

According to the most recent version of the Diagnostic and Statistical Manual of Mental Disorders (DSM-IV-TR), there are three patterns of behavior that indicate ADHD. People with ADHD may show several types of being continually inattentive. They may have a pattern of being hyperactive and impulsive far more than others of their age. Or they may show all three types of behavior. This means that there are three subtypes of ADHD recognized by professionals. They are the inattentive, hyperactive-impulsive type, and the combined type. (that does not show significant and hyperactive-impulsive symptoms)

N. More than manage. ...disorder, and the combined type. (that displays both inattentive and hyperactive-impulsive symptoms)

Hyperactive type

Hyperactive children always seem to be "on the go" or constantly in motion. They dash around touching or playing with whatever is in sight, or talk incessantly. Sitting still at dinner or during a school lesson or story can be a difficult task. They squirm and fidget in their seats or roam around the room. Or they may wriggle their feet, touch everything, or noisily tap their pencil. Hyperactive teenagers or adults may feel internally restless. They often report they

R. Now. ...need to stay busy and may try to do several things at once.

Impulsive children seem unable to curb their immediate reactions or think before they act. They will often blurt out inappropriate comments, display their emotions without restraint, and act without regard for the later consequences of their conduct. Their impulsivity may make it hard for them to wait for things they want or to take their turn in games. They may grab a toy from another child or hit when they're upset. Even as teenagers or adults they may impulsively choose to do things that have an immediate but small payoff rather than engage in activities that may take more effort yet provide much greater but delayed rewards.

R. He does very well. ...are

* Feeling restless, often fidgeting with hands or feet, or squirming while seated
* Running, climbing, or leaving a seat in situations where sitting or quiet behavior is expected
* Blurting out answers before hearing the whole question
* Having difficulty waiting in line or taking turns

N. He does very, very, very well. ...the ball on the way to write down an assignment, or leave it at school. They will forget to bring a book home, or bring the wrong one. The homework, if finally finished, is full of errors and erasures. Homework is particularly hard for these children. They will forget to write down an assignment, or leave it at school. They will forget to bring a book home, or bring the wrong one. The homework, if finally finished, is full of errors and erasures.

R. So, who knows. of inattention

* Often becoming easily distracted by irrelevant sights and sounds
* Often failing to pay attention to details and making careless mistakes
* Rarely following instructions carefully and completely losing or forgetting things like toys, or pencils, books, and tools needed for a task
* Often skipping from one uncompleted activity to another

Children diagnosed with the Predominantly Inattentive Type of ADHD are seldom impulsive or hyperactive, yet they have significant problems paying attention. They appear to be daydreaming, "spacey," easily confused, slow moving, and lethargic. They may have difficulty processing information as quickly and accurately as other children. When the teacher gives oral or even written instructions, this child has a hard time understanding what he or she is supposed to do and makes frequent mistakes. Yet the child may sit quietly, unobtrusively, and even appear to be working but not fully attending to or understanding the task and the instructions.

These children don't show significant problems with impulsivity and overactivity in the classroom, on the school ground, or at home. They may get along better with other children than the more impulsive and hyperactive types of ADHD, and they may not have the same sorts of social problems so common with the combined type of ADHD. So often their problems with inattention are overlooked. But they need help just as much as children with other types of ADHD, who cause more obvious problems in the classroom.

Y. [64]

Owns (with S.[65]):

A minivan.

A cellphone.

He owns (with S.) $80,000 of a $200,000 house.

He owns rugs, chairs, TVs, and knives and forks. Computers. Pillowcases.

Y. owns a 401(k), a Roth IRA, and mutual funds.

College plans for the kids (at 20K each).

He doesn't own the dog. You don't own family.

Ditto for the kids, though Y. says to them, You're mine.

It means he loves them.

Pause.

138

Y. owns torn cartilage in his ribs and periodontal disease and plantar fasciitis and stiffening knuckles and an irritable bowel.[66]

---

[66] Lomotil®

The diphenoxylate portion of this drug is used to treat diarrhea, while the atropine relieves muscle spasms in the gut. Common side effects include headache, dizziness, drowsiness, blurred vision, dry mouth, and constipation. Although it is not a narcotic, diphenoxylate is derived from narcotics and may be mildly habit-forming. Diphenoxylate/atropine is typically prescribed to control diarrhea in the short-term, and is not recommended for long-term use. <http://ibdcrohns.about.com/cs/faqsibs/a/ibsfaq_3.htm>

Y.

Likes:

Wind-up toys.

Pewter paperweights.

He likes driving home from work.

He likes foods with salt.[67] Olives and pickles. Liverwurst and limburger cheese, which offend the kids.

He likes the goofy elegance of a good fondue and Zippo® lighters and patent leather shoes.

Y. likes that family holidays include shelled nuts and lit fireplaces and watching TV.

---

[67] Types of antihypertensive drugs

- Diuretics: These drugs help your body get rid of extra sodium and fluid so that your blood vessels don't have to hold so much fluid.
- Beta blockers: These drugs block the effects of adrenaline.
- Alpha blockers: These drugs help your blood vessels stay open.
- ACE inhibitors: These drugs prevent your blood vessels from constricting by blocking your body from making angiotensin II. Angiotensin II is a chemical that constricts blood vessels.
- Calcium channel blockers: These drugs help prevent your blood vessels from constricting by blocking calcium from entering your cells.
- Combinations: These drugs combine an ACE inhibitor with a calcium channel blocker.

<http://familydoctor.org/092.xml>

He likes baggy underwear and a good crap. Picking dead skin off his toes.

Y. likes that S. puts aside money for car repairs and a new water heater and things the kids want.

He likes that his parents need him.

And the same for the kids.

Though it makes him tired, and sometimes he says it's all too much.

That could never be, which Y. likes.

—

Y.

Wants:

For nothing.[68]

Small stuff—

Reading in bed in the morning.
A back massage.
The absence of dust.
A decent haircut.
Shoes that fit.
New foods.

Time to travel. And for D.[69] and D.[70] to come without a fight.

Y. wants no fighting at all. Y. never wants to again hear a human call another human a turd.

Y. wants the love of his kids.

To feel more about his parents' struggle with small tasks.

That they gave him more time, once.

To stop thinking their moment has passed.

---

[68] Though, really, he wants to continue not wanting (much).

[69] Dependent

[70] Dependent

Breathe.

Y. wants his children to choose interesting things over what's not.

But for them to be safe. Because the world, after all....

Y. wants his dog to live forever.

And to be able to smoke again.[71]

To be rude sometimes.

It's not much, is it?

---

[71] At night, he chews **Nicorette**®.

Y.

Feels:

A little scared.

He says, Is Tupac any good?

He says, Two-Pack, and D. laughs.

Y. can't name comedians on late-night shows.

Y. feels sick about four-hundred-dollar video game systems, though they bought one.

He feels unsure. Things he knew, to the kids they don't register. They've never seen *The Love Boat*. D. gives him a look.

What?

Y. feels stupid worrying over what's cool.

There's no cool in the *NewsHour with Jim Lehrer*. No cool in mortgages. No cool in dieting.[72] There's no cool in getting a good deal on tires. There's no cool in drinking a martini or two every night. That's habitual, it seems, and kind of sad.

---

[72] The **SEROTRIM®** Weight Loss Program provides the optimal balance of carbohydrates to naturally raise brain serotonin levels. As brain serotonin levels increase, people experience increased satiety and a sense of overall well-being. <http://www.serotrim.com>

There's no cool in self-pitying jokes about your own lack of cool.

Silence.

Look, Y. says, I don't want to be young. I just don't want to be old. Being old, he says. Unless you're rich, he says, it means you eat shit. You're too tired to fight. You're supposed to know more, but you know less. I feel like.

You accept a decent wage, if it means comfort. You follow national politics. You play golf.

Fuck all this, Y. says. I'm not dead, yet.

The kids hate when Y. says fuck. That makes him feel good.

S. tells him to put a sock in it.

Y.

Expects:

The worst.

He expects the day when the kids won't visit. Not for holidays. Not ever.

No birthday cards.

Y. expects to die, alone, in a diaper, in a home, on Medicaid (**see endnote**).

Or the kids will move back for good.

Or his money will roll out, for graduate school and apartments in expensive cities. Vehicles. New homes. Grandchildren.

Not grandchildren. Y. expects that if he expects them, he'll get none.

Or Y. expects D. will sacrifice herself for a job, and a marriage, a house, and kids. He expects she'll take shit from her husband. He'll be told it's none of his business.

He expects D. and D. will hate him for thinking of himself. For once putting them in daycare. For letting them watch TV.

For not letting them watch TV.

Y. expects his hairline will recede to his bald spot.

He expects to work forever, because he expects retirement will be only a tedious step toward death.

He expects that if he ever retires S. will leave.

He can't say why, but he expects that anyway, when raising kids ends.

Maybe that never happens.

Y.

Knows:

He should have become a forest ranger.

Or opened his own business.

He knows there's no hell like working for another person.

He should be the guy in the know.

Y. knows that Bill, at work, hates him. Y. knows sometimes people won't like you.

He knows it helps if they do.

Y. knows it's all in how you look at it.

Y. knows that being a man doesn't mean being manly, but he still knows the pleasure of:

- Camping
- Farting
- Mixing drinks

Y. knows he should talk with D. about sex.

Or D.[73] That he doesn't know. How it's done these days?

---

[73] Nonoxynol-9 What Is It? Spermicides come in several different forms: cream, gel, foam, film, and suppositories.

He knows he should care more about S.'s feelings.

More at least than he cares about D.'s or D.'s. About which he cares a lot.

But that's not so easy. She doesn't care about his.

Y. knows that's not true. He knows it's a cliché.

As is he.

Most spermicides contain nonoxynol-9, a chemical that kills sperm. Spermicides can be used alone but are more effective when used with another method of birth control such as a _condom_ or diaphragm. <http://kidshealth.org/teen/sexual_health/contraception_spermicide.html>

Y.

Only really Hates:

The word hate.

The kids hate so many things.

But it's just what they say.

So he does, too.

He hates waiting, and wasting time.

Chores.

He hates picking up people's shoes and books and dirty cups.

Rudeness.

Stupidity.

Y. hates himself for being impatient and judgmental.

He hates complainers.

Hypocrites.

The perpetually unaware.

Mildew.

Drivers who don't follow the rules.

The feel of wool hats.

Pushiness.

Y. hates hates hates when S. runs down his folks.

There's a thin line between love and hate.

Y. hates clichés.

And the wart on his toe. That thing Y. fucking hates.[74]

---

[74] To treat plantar warts, you'll need a 40 percent Salicylic Acid solution or patch, which peels off the infected skin a little bit at a time.

Y.

Forgets:

Mailing bills. To buy ketchup, or gas.

To back up his hard drive.

And:

When D. walked. Her first words.

He forgets to write things down so he won't forget.

He forgets the names of college friends.

The names of the kids' friends.

He forgets what it's like to be a kid.

To be more like his mother than his father.

He forgets himself and yells. Picks his nose.

He forgets to listen to S. Why.

They're not great friends.

Y. forgets when.

What.

Forgets the feeling of loneliness.

How much it hurts to fall hard or break a bone.

He forgets making mistakes.

Y. forgets losing control. Maybe saying the wrong thing. Then it happens.

Then he forgets again.[75]

---

[75] Y. forgets when he first needed something to smooth himself out.

Selective Serotonin Reuptake Inhibitors (SSRIs): Which is best?

<www.biopsychiatry.com/ssris.htm>

Y.

Imagines:

Piercing his nipples.

Shaving his head.

Sweating in a sauna.

Y. imagines putting his face in the hairy cracks of fat women.

Squatting of all sorts.

Y. imagines his wife spread under a wiry man with a prominent jaw.

Surrounding himself with soft machines that move his limbs.

Being hit in the face.

The viciousness of fishhooks.

Falling from a height.

The redness of embarrassed skin.

Moist smells.

Covering himself in sticky foods.

Using drugs.[76]

Acting badly.

Y. can't imagine others don't imagine these things, too.

---

[76] Sifted from leaves and buds and pressed into cakes (**Hashish**).

Y.

Hopes:

For nothing bad.

No one hurt or sick.

Y. hopes for the kids.

That they marry late.

Y. tells them that people should live.

Grow up when you're thirty, he says.

Not much later, he says.

He hopes they're always nice to their mom.

And happy, whatever that means.

And that they don't lie to him.

Like he hopes they don't lie to him now. Much.

He hopes they don't lie to him too much. That they go to the movies when they go to the movies.

Y. hopes he doesn't love D. more than D. or D. more than D.

And what about S.

Y. hopes she still loves him.

That they'll know how to live when the kids move out. That maybe it'll be good, for a while. And then.

Y. hopes to die of a coronary while running in the woods. No surgeries or softening bones. Mush for brains.

Y. hopes for a big heart attack.

But not for a while yet.

There's more to come.

Endnote

O.[77]

(Aleve®, ex-lax®, Tambocor®)

Jean said it would be for the best if I sold the house and moved
in with the Sisters, and I said, I don't know. I live here. Fifty
years, I said. I'm in the house fifty years, with Daniel. I don't
think so, I said, and Jean said, But Daniel's gone. Like I didn't
know. So I said, He's here while I am, and she put on her face,
and I wished I hadn't asked her. But I didn't want her mad,
and I said, I know he's gone, honey, and I'm thankful for my
friends, which she thought on, looking at the floor. O., she
said, there's only so much, she said. And you gave up the car,
she said. She said, You're gonna need to hire someone.

She said, You're gonna have to find a new place sometime.

She said the Sisters could give me a private room, maybe a
corner spot, with windows. She said you can bring your own
bed, if you want, and your dresser, and chairs, and whatever
fits. You get your own bathroom.

---

[77] Outpatient

I said to Jean, Does my door lock?

It depends, she said, and I said, On what?

Safety, she said.

You get your privacy, Jean said. Don't worry.

There's Faye and Marty, I said, and Annie. They don't mind going to the store. Annie said she likes spending the time.

We are an aging country. And all of a sudden all those things that we take for granted every day, like driving or cleaning our home, going out shopping—the natural aging process does begin to make those things more difficult. And how our society, or how our communities have been structured—either with or without sidewalks and traffic signals that may be a lot better for freshmen in college than for a senior citizen—begins to point out a big issue here. That is, as a nation we are not prepared for longer life. And so the transportation issue points to larger questions: How will we work? How will we play? How will we get around? How will we live tomorrow now that we live longer? —Joe Coughlin, MIT Aging Lab

But Jean said they have their lives. What if they're on vacation, she said, or one of them gets sick, and she came over on the sofa and put her hand on my knee, and she said, I can't be driving over here all the time now, she said, with my job.

O., she said, so I put my hand on hers, to stop her. Her fingers felt fat.

Honey, I said, I'm grateful for my friends. Every day, I said, I thank God for them.

P.[78]

(Forteo®, Calcitonin, Celebrex®, Betadine® Swabs, Lactaid®)

I had colds, and I had flu, and a couple times a stomach bug. Only needed the hospital, though, for the boys, for C.'s[79] tonsils, and when C.[80] cut his head. They gave him a dozen stitches. Cut his hair off.

D.[81] stayed when they took his gallbladder, and twice for his heart. Then his back problems, and then till he passed, God bless him. Last time, they tied his arms down, because of the needles. They must have hurt, the needles.

My teeth gave me some problems, when I was little, but it was bother, not sick, and I never had cholesterol or high blood pressure or thyroid. Worst for me, I can't drink milk. When I want ice cream, I take a pill.

In an average year, more than 250,000 older Americans suffer fractured hips, at a cost in excess of $10 billion. More than 90 percent of hip fractures are associated with falls, and most of these fractures occur in persons more than 70 years of age. It is projected that more than 340,000 hip fractures will occur on average in coming years, and this incidence is expected to double by the middle of the 21st century.

One fourth of elderly persons who sustain a hip fracture die within six months of the injury. More than 50 percent of older patients who survive hip fractures are discharged to a nursing home, and nearly one half of these patients are still in a nursing home one year later. —American Academy of Family Physicians

Garibedian cut out a lump, which turned out it was a cyst, so I said, Just leave them in. I'll come in if it's cancer, I said, because I'll know. You know with something like that.

---

[78] Patient

[79] Child

[80] Child

[81] Deceased

But C. hired the nurse, for peace of mind, he said, and C. and his wife bought the monitor for when the girl was off. I told them I'd wear it, but I didn't, because the cord itched. I'd crawl to the phone again, if I had to.

The girl, though, she told C. I didn't keep the sores clean, and she said I wouldn't walk, which was a lie. She said she needed to come full-time, for a while, if someone couldn't stay, which C. couldn't, because of the kids. Talked herself out of a job, because C. told her I might should be in a facility, if I needed that kind of care, and she said she figured, maybe. She didn't seem too smart, I said to him, and rude after she first came, and he said, Well, okay, then, and he found me a spot with the Sisters, and he said it made him feel better, and C., too.

I didn't say anything, except he knew best, C. did, and I knew it was a cost.

I don't mind the company. Sister Patty and Sister Claudine come and sit. I've got my TV, and I like walking inside, though most mornings I say, No, because I'd rather stay in bed a bit. I don't feel so good, I say to the Sisters, but I don't feel too bad, either. I'll get up later, I tell them, God willing, if they don't make a fuss.

I.[82]

(Inderal®, Haldol®)

I sing, for Sister Margaret. She says, Just sing. Don't wait on pilgrims, so I start, Gather 'round me, everybody, gather 'round me while I'm preachin', feel a sermon comin' on me, the topic will be sin and that's what I'm ag'in', and a couple folks come at the door. I don't remember them in the group. Sister Margaret says, I., your friends are here. Sister Margaret says I should finish later. Well, I say to the big girl, I wish I'd known, I'd have been ready, and she says, Sister Margaret marked it, and, then, I., you look fine, dear. It's just lunch, she says. Susan, she says. Remember? And Stephen, she says, and he smiles. I'm singing, I say, and Sister Margaret tells me I should wait till later, anyway, when more folks will come. If it's for the best, I say, and I ask Susan how she feels, and about folks at home, though she says I mean the people on Mission Hill, not Sunridge, which I don't, and I tell her I don't want to share a room. I ordered a single. I ordered a single, I say, again, to her, and to Margaret, and I say, I know

> Polypharmacy, very common in the elderly, and the possibility of drug-drug interactions must be considered as a cause of agitation. Medications such as benzodiazepines (Xanax®), beta-blockers (Propranolol®), selective serotonin reuptake inhibitors (Zoloft®), neuroleptics (Thorazine®) and diphenhydramine (Benadryl®) can cause problems. —American Psychiatric Association

> The U.S. Food and Drug Administration has not approved any medication for the treatment of behavioral agitation in dementia. However, the first line of defense is usually a traditional major tranquilizer such as haloperidol (Haldol®), thioridazine (Mellaril®), thiothixene (Navane®) or perphenazine (Etrafon®, Trilafon®). —H. Michael Zal, D.O., F.A.P.A.

---

[82] Inpatient

where to find my room. Anywhere else, I say, it was visiting. I knew which was mine. I knew which things were mine. Except now. There's a lady, I tell Susan. She lies on my bed. My bed, I say, and she smells like number two. My bed, I say, so I put my pictures in the middle of it, which showed her. Let me put on my hair, I say to Susan, before we go, and the Sister says, Dear, we gave them away, because of the state, and I say, What state, I say, and Sister Margaret says to the big girl, They don't allow the wigs. Let her sing. It calms her, and Susan says it's time to go, and the man puts his hand on my elbow, and we go in the hall. Susan, I say, quiet, so the Sister won't hear, let's get out of here. Let's get out of here, I say, and she says, Okay. We're going.

DNR[83]

(Salbutamol® by metered aerosol or 2.5-5 mg by nebuliser, q4-6h; Glycopyrrolate 0.2-0.4mg SC, ± repeat at 30min, then q4-6h or 0.6-1.2mg/24h CSCI0; Clonazepam 0.5 mg SL or SC q12h or 1-2 mg/24h CSCI and titrate; 9% Sodium chloride; Morphine)

They try to feed her.

She ate with her hands.

She doesn't eat now.

They give her broth.

Q: Are there any beneficial effects of dehydration?

[83] Do Not Resuscitate

Popsicles.

She sucks on a straw.

They give her an IV.
If she drinks some.

Not if she stops.

They stop the IV.

It's what they do.

Unless the fam-
ily says no.

under
other

She doesn't have any.

the

The second husband's
kid gets what's left.

when
coming

There's nothing left.

Costs five thou-
sand a month.

i

From her savings.

i

Medicare pays now.

i don't

They auctioned
her things.

my

Said they'd give
us notice.

then
the boys

A first look.

But we found out
from the paper.

arms

Like everyone else.

and

She had some nice
Hummels®.

turn

We go see her.

the

A: Dehydration can
actually have several
potential benefits for a
person who is at the end
stages of his/her life:

* Secretions in the lungs
are diminished, so cough
and congestion are less.

* Dehydration can lead
to a melting away of the
swelling and increased
comfort in a person
who has edema (swell-
ing of the body caused
by excess body fluids)
or ascites (fluid in the
abdominal cavity).

* With dehydration,
there is less fluid in the
gastrointestinal tract,
which may decrease
nausea, vomiting, bloat-
ing and regurgitation.

—American Hos-
pice Foundation

166

when

it's

so

i

maybe
day

when

i don't

i don't

We used to go.

Got so she didn't
know us.

We go sometimes.

They say it's just us.

It's close.

We'll try to go.

They've got la-
dies who sit.

Maybe she can tell.

You don't know.

She's just bones.

She kept some
Christmas figures.

Said they'd give
us notice.

Us being neighbors.

And friends.

Seems like we're it.

Poor thing.

God bless.

For patients at end of life
who are unable to com-
municate and who have
not documented their
treatment preferences,
medical decisions are usually made by an individual
physician, close friend, or
acquaintance. —*Journal
of Clinical Oncology*